D0463499

S.P. O'Farrell

SIMONE LAFRAY

and the
Chocolatiers' Ball

Brandylane
Publishers, Inc.
Publishing books since 1985

ISBN: 978-1-947860-34-6

LCCN: 2019931246

Cover illustrated by Kelly O'Neill
Cover and interior designed by Michael Hardison
Project managed by Christina Kann

Cover fonts: Cambria, Chennai Slab, Parisish
Interior fonts: Adobe Caslon Pro and Qokijo

Printed in the United States of America

Published by
Brandlane Publishers
5 S. 1st Street
Richmond, Virginia 23219
brandylanepublishers.com

Brandylane
Publishers, Inc.
Publishing books since 1985

This book is dedicated to

Arielle Bowen

(a.k.a. Simone LaFray)

And to avid readers
and secret keepers everywhere—

STAY STRONG.

*Thank you to my mother, Jane,
who proofread and corrected
all of my lousy English papers.*

*To my "funnest" friend, Brendan
—I'm thinking Geneva.*

*And to my wife, Emily:
This book shines because of you.*

*Thank you to my team at Brandylane Publishers;
Annie Tobey, Christina Kann, Michael Hardison,
and Robert Pruett. I am grateful for you all.*

Overture

"**B**onjour," or should I say, "Hello."

The evening Mother caught me finishing her copy of *Moby Dick*, the fact was not lost on her that it was my fourth birthday. What did strike her as odd was that the book had only been missing since lunchtime. She asked that I kindly return it to her bookshelf in the morning, which I did. I was done with it.

In my twelve years of experience, I have concluded that adults invariably underestimate children and gravitate to two types: the precocious, oh-so-sweet girl with curly hair and full eyelashes (that's my sister and you'll meet her soon enough) and the doey-eyed, athletic boy who is revered for simply being in attendance and not burping loudly. I can assure you that I bear no resemblance to either, although these tenets have served me well in my occupation.

If we were to pass on the sidewalk or share a seat on the transit, you wouldn't notice me—I wouldn't let you. If you did happen to catch a glance, the image would quickly fade: a typical girl, practically invisible among the crowd. Straight brown hair, glasses, bookish, gray knits, blah, seemingly ordinary in every way—but that's what I want you to see. The truth might alarm you.

I know we just met, but I have a secret to tell. In fact, I have two, but I'm not comfortable sharing the other. And besides, it's been of no help to me thus far. You will agree that the first is far more relevant. Simply put, I'm an *espion*, or a spy, and the most promising agent within the Ministry of Foreign Affairs, or so I'm told. I have no reason to discredit this assertion as I was destined to one day walk in my mother's rather large footsteps. However, no one expected it to happen this early, not even her. Ratted out by a white whale. Since I could crawl, Mother has told me that the truly strong are silent and serve without applause. I prefer it this way.

Her wisdom comes from experience, as Mother is no typical mademoiselle. After 15 years of decorated service in the French Army, she now works within the Ministry. Her official title is "Diplomat," but she is perhaps the most accomplished spy in the world. She is a legend within the community, a patriot, and my hero. I'm the luckiest girl in the world to be the daughter of the one-and-only Cpt. Julia C. LaFray.

As for me, I can remember every second of my life since my first birthday—all five senses heightened in a constant flutter, every detail absorbed and analyzed. You get used to it, although it can be exhausting. Perhaps my most remarkable skill was hiding it from others. They didn't need to know, and they wouldn't understand. My mother was the only one who could see me—well, most of me—and she told my father when she thought he was ready. He took the news well.

I'm comfortable with the fact that I have never been picked for a schoolyard game at the Elizabeth of Trinity School for Girls, although I'm surprisingly athletic and I never draw attention to myself. Never ever. Trinity would have a series of junior league football titles—sorry, I meant soccer titles—by now had Coach Rousseau picked me for the old red and white. She prefers the aforementioned oh-so-sweet girls, which has produced a perennial gaggle of perfectly braided, ribbon adorned ponytails and unstained uniforms. It is safe to say that Trinity will not be making space for the City Cup any time soon.

Growing up in Paris with a secret was the ideal life, although circumstances were about to change. They can't be averted; certain wheels are now in motion that are beyond my control. I'm afraid an unwelcome light is about to illuminate the comfortable shadows where I'm most at ease.

My apologies—where are my manners? We have not been formally introduced. I am, truly, Simone LaFray.

The Invisible Girl

Summer mornings in Paris were perfect. The days were warm, inviting, and exciting. I woke up every morning thinking that anything was possible: a museum tour, a view of the city from that tower, or maybe a helicopter ride to a secured location in Germany to crunch data. I preferred the last, although that particular morning started like most others—quietly sitting in Prentice Park, watching my sister roam the lawns in a flock of warbling seven-year-olds, each trying to outdo the others through forced laughter, dramatic pronouncements, and toothless smiles that usually simmer into a lawn sideshow of some sort. It appeared that *The Three Little Pigs* was in pre-production.

"This book was better the second time," I whispered to myself as my eyes rolled over the page and my left hand scribbled notes into its margins. The first time I read *The Count of Monte Cristo*, I was on a train to Zurich and found the alpine highlands to be far more interesting. The second time I read it, I was parked at one of my sister's extended ballet recitals. There were no distractions that time.

"Ugh. This hair," I murmured to myself while guiding it away from my eyes. It was now barely long enough to tuck behind my ears, although I wished it was short again. Long hair was such a pain, but Mother said I should give it a try. I was not convinced.

Listening for the sound of Mia's voice as my eyes rolled through another page, I could tell that she had once again assumed the roles of lead actor and special effects coordinator. A quick glance up to confirm, but she was running toward me with our dog Gigi in tow. She wanted something.

Dressed in a vibrant yellow dress and red-striped sweater, she stopped with both hands on her knees. The dress, which was perfectly pressed and unsoiled, had been a birthday present from our Aunt Emma last month. As she straightened up, her curly blonde hair cascaded off her shoulders, and a smile emerged. I have to admit, she was beautiful, even at seven years old.

"Simone, why won't you play with us? Gigi keeps barking and running off with our props." Mia looked back to find her friends staging the next act and was visibly miffed that they were proceeding without her. She turned back to me with a huff. "We need a wolf," she added with a growing sense of mischief.

"Ten more minutes, Mia. Then we need to go," I said, looking over the top of my book. To avoid any response from her, I quickly lowered my eyes, pulled the hair out of my face again, and turned the page. She growled at me and kicked a smoothed stone off the ground and into a nearby bush. An unsuspecting squirrel darted out, attracting the attention of Gigi, who proceeded to chase it up a nearby oak. Gigi circled the tree twice with great expectations of a new playmate, although she soon gave up and found a crooked stick to pounce on.

"You never play with us," Mia whined at me as she began to mellow. I dared not answer. I knew that she wanted to return to her friends more than plead for my involvement, so I continued to ignore her. After another ten seconds of awkward silence, she shrugged her shoulders, turned, and ran. Returning with the now well-worn stick, our small but stout bulldog dashed after her.

Just a hint of the morning dew remained, leaving a faint outline of Mia's pathway back to her troupe. When she settled back into the group, I re-surveyed the lawn, smelled the air—no street vendors yet—and noticed that the smooth, dark face of my watch was blinking. Issued to me from the ministry, this was no ordinary watch, and to call it *smart* or *high-tech* underserves its capabilities.

Don't let the weathered blue and red canvas band fool you. I tapped the center of the face four times, drew the shape of a triangle, then a circle, then another triangle. I lowered my hand behind the book and its face flashed to life.

"Good morning, dear. Still at the park?" said a warm voice.

"Good morning, Mother. Where are you?' I whispered. When Mother was away on assignment, I never knew her whereabouts, and I silently scolded myself for even asking. It was unprofessional. Wherever she was, the day was ending, and she had a mild sunburn on her cheeks.

"Well," she offered, trying not to embarrass me for asking, "I'm safe and sound here, but we'll be going silent for the next four or five days. I wanted you to know."

"Oh? Nothing serious I hope," I said with a tinge of apprehension.

"No, just business," she confidently stated. Her eyes relaxed, and she tilted her head just slightly to take a closer look at me. "You look tired, Simone. Does Father have you working too hard?" she asked with the gentle delivery of an adoring mother. I could almost feel the warmth of her palm on my cheek.

"No, I'm fine. I was up late last night reading. That's all." In fact, I *was* up late reading, but that's nothing new. Sleeping is highly overrated.

"I see. Well, try to get some rest today," she replied. Her eyes tracked to something in front of her and it was apparent that our conversation would be short-lived. "My love to you all, dear. Stay strong," and with that, the tiny screen went black and my mind began to race.

"She's in Singapore. I know she's in Singapore," I whispered. I wanted to be in Singapore. *I was in Berlin a month ago, and now I'm sitting here on a bench looking at my sister playing with her friends. I hope Mom gets home soon*, I thought as I tried to find any little bit of margin left to write on.

Exactly 47 seconds later, a spirited discussion between Mia and her best friend, Riley H. Swanson, broke out over what can only be described as "creative differences." This occurred almost every morning, and after an attending mother brokered a peace treaty, all was right again and Mia assumed the role as director.

At this point, caught in another rerun of a typical morning at the park, I lost interest, and my thoughts returned to Mother. "Singapore?" I murmured. My mind recounted every aspect of the discussion; the angle of the low sunlight on her face, the background noise, the faint reflections on her eyes, everything. I rewound it several times, and—*Wait, that was Thai dialect in the background, not Chinese. She's not in Singapore.* My mind went over it again, but faster still, and again. Then it hit. *She's in Bangkok; it has to be Bangkok*, I said to myself with some level of self-satisfaction. Seeking a new focal point, my eyes settled back on Mia and I started to tap my feet impatiently.

"Boring. Nothing exciting ever happens here, and how can she just *act* in front of all those people? All those eyes on you, watching every movement, hanging on every word." I shuddered as a cold twinge crept up my neck.

"What if she messes up? What if it's not any good?"

I checked my fingernails, which were chewed to the quick, and suddenly a wave of unwelcome anxiety came over me. The thought of being the center of attention was paralyzing. My breathing hastened, but then, thankfully, a cool breeze passed by and my mind reset.

Recalibrating myself, I instinctively moved my eyes over to a break in a hedge and I counted quietly to myself, "Three, two, one—" and a smartly dressed lady sprung through with a large dog.

Right on time. And a red hat today? I said to myself with a final inscription going into the book. Balance had returned, and I found the old wooden bench to be once again comfortable.

Three minutes later, the makeshift production ended with a chorus of huffs and puffs. The giggling cast bowed to the point of exhaustion as the mothers started to collect an assortment of backpacks, stuffed animals, and toys that had been scattered about.

"Finally," I said to myself. The sun was now warm on my face and our morning at the park was drawing to an end.

I stood up and clapped softly as Mia skipped towards me.

"See you later, Mia!" shouted one of her disbanding cast mates.

My eyes tracked to the source, although I didn't turn my head. "Who's that girl with Mia? Is that her sister?" asked the girl's mother. I turned my back to them, but my ears focused intently.

"Um, I'm not sure. It might be her cousin or something. I don't know," the girl answered. Casually I turned and caught a quick glance of the girl scraping mud off her shoe. "I think her name is Camille, or maybe—uh—can we get a snack on the way home?"

Do I look like a Camille? I thought. I threw *The Count of Monte Cristo* into my backpack and clipped on Gigi's red leather leash. It was time to go.

As Mia zigzagged across the lawn pretending to be a buzzing bee in front of me, I looked up and spotted a large cloud gliding over. The cloud had no particular shape or coloring, but I had to stare for just a second. The moment was interrupted when I walked out of the sunshine and into the spotty shade. My skin relaxed subtly to the slight drop in temperature and my shoes were getting splashed with each step across the heavier wet grass.

I love Prentice Park, even when it's boring. I love the trees, the bushes, the grass, the sculptures, everything. Only the seasons changed its look, but the park itself remained constant, permanent, and comforting. With another step, I smelled warming bread, frying onions, and sweet calissons pluming from the vending carts outside the wall. "Right on time," I whispered.

As we passed through the metal gates and onto the smoothed

brick sidewalk, Mia was reliving her performance, while my mind was sorting out the details of the morning. "Mr. Dubois brought an umbrella today, but there was no rain in the forecast. And Mrs. Mormond, who always walks her dog Cleo between 9:30 and 9:40, didn't arrive until 9:53. Why did Mr. Dubois bring an umbrella? And why was Mrs. Mormond late? There must be some explanation." These and about ten other thoughts swirled in my head.

Moving away from the gate, I could not help but notice a man on a bench turning a crisp morning copy of *Corriere della Sera. You don't see that every day*, I thought, but what stuck out most was a small shock of vibrant red hair rising above the fold. As we passed, a page turned, casually masking his face, but that hair—it was as if his head was on fire.

"Come on, Simone!" Mia shouted back at me. Mia took every opportunity to shout at me in public, especially when I was causing her some inconvenience. She knew it made me uncomfortable, but that's what little sisters do.

I turned to her, and the man shuffled his paper slightly, almost signaling some acknowledgment. Maybe I was overanalyzing this, but I did need to catch up. Both Mia and Gigi have a proclivity to wander on the way home. Who can blame them? It's Paris.

By the middle of the next block, the sun was back in my face and the collar of my shirt was driving me crazy. The city was awake now. Shops were open, people were moving with purpose, and the volume of the city was rising. Mia started to run to the next corner with Gigi closely behind. An essential component of our morning was about to take place as a beaming smile was waiting for us.

"Bonjour, girls," a large man shouted to us. "How was your performance today?" he added through his wild beard.

Mia never wasted the opportunity to take center stage, so she snapped to attention and said, "My best to date, Monsieur Jake." Jacque Otto St. Marin, or simply "Jake," had been selling newspapers on this corner for as long as I could remember. He was consistently overdressed for his occupation and had an almost clown-like air about him. He was as much a part of our walk home as the sidewalks and streets. No matter how busy he was, he always had time to say, "Bonjour."

As Mia described her performance, my mind gravitated to a large blue and white newspaper delivery truck that had stopped just three meters in front of us. I noticed the delivery man move to the back of his truck and was curious about what he might be dropping off.

"Monsieur Jake, what time is it?" I overheard Mia ask with a sly smile. Jake had an old pocket watch that she usually asked to see. He always obliged, as it was a family heirloom and a source of great pride. She had seen it a million times, but Jake relished the opportunity to present it in grand fashion.

He was pulling it out of his vest pocket, when Gigi barked at the delivery man, who was dropping a large pile of papers.

"Sorry to be running late with these, Jake," the man said as he turned to jump back in his truck. Turning to acknowledge him, Monsieur Jake fumbled the watch off the chain and into the air. I noticed it spinning in the air and had to do something—I couldn't let it hit the sidewalk—so with surgical precision I slid forward with my hand outstretched, pinching its crown between my two fingers just before it hit the ground. I stood up without straightening my clothes and handed it back to a temporarily distracted Jake. "It's 10:26, Mia, we need to go," I said plainly.

"Why, thank you, Simone. It just—well," he said to me while he inspected the pocket watch for damage. There was none. "Thank goodness. I'll have to get this chain fixed," he added, reattaching it to the chain.

Thankfully, in the next second, two men in business suits walked up and one said, "Bonjour. Two papers, please."

Mia gave a frown as Jake's attention was diverted. She would not hold the watch today. I gave Mia a little nudge and said, "Let's go already."

As we continued to weave through the fifteenth district, the day took on a normal feel. "Remember that we have to stop by Uncle Giles' office to pick up Father's papers," said Mia to me as she peered into a hat shop.

"Of course, I remember, Mia. It's Tuesday," I replied.

During the summer, we often stopped by the accounting office of Giles LaFray to bring home paperwork. Although we called him "uncle," Giles was our father's first cousin, and he had built a notable business comprised primarily of bakeries, pâtisseries, confectionaries, and other food-related businesses. He was reputable, exceedingly smart, and discreet with all business affairs, although I can't remember him ever coming over for dinner.

As we turned a corner and made our way down Rue Strate, my eyes tracked to an opening art gallery. This storefront had been vacant for weeks, but today it was alive with inventory and splashes of vibrant colors. Shabby sculptures and old paintings sat outside in heaps. As we approached, I could not help but stare and try to catalog the image in my mind.

"Bonjour," said the storekeeper as we approached. The tall woman was dressed in a checkered dress and had her curly black hair pulled back by a red and white scarf.

I politely replied, "Bonjour, Mademoiselle," but made no eye contact. I desperately wanted to ask about the store, but it would have to wait. As I passed by the front door, the crackling voice of Edith Piaf cascaded out and stopped me for just a second. Father played me the same record when I was younger.

"I have got to come back here," I said to myself.

Now, only four doors down was Giles' office. A small, perfectly level, black and white sign hung in the front window that read,

"LaFray's Comptable Services." The stoop was always swept and the mail slot polished. The front door was heavy and old. I helped Mia open it and the sound of a faint distant buzzer could be heard. In front of us was an elevated dark counter with a metal desk fan that moved from side to side. There was nothing on the counter except for the fan and a dish that held five business cards. It always contained five business cards; no more, no less.

"Good morning, girls," said an approaching voice. "Is your dog with you this week?"

"Yes, sir. She's with us, but we left her outside," we said in unison.

With no sense of occasion and in an unbroken stride, Giles LaFray glided to the back of the counter. He looked past us to confirm that Gigi was in fact outside, then stood up straight. After adjusting his bow tie, he tried to conjure something conversational to say, but nothing came out.

"I don't know how Louie—I mean, your father—can allow that dog to play about in his store all day," he said as he placed a large envelope on the counter. He made eye contact with me to make sure I was paying attention, then made a notation on his ledger. This was the same envelope that we picked up every week. No folds, creases, or stains, only a hand-typed label that read *LaFray's Comptable Services*.

As soon as I grabbed the package, he turned and started to walk back down the hall. "Remind your father that I will be stopping in tomorrow at 2:00. We have business to discuss," he said as his voice trailed off. He added, "I'm sure he has forgotten," just before closing his door.

With Giles back in his office, I took a second to look at his walls, which had been recently painted. The fading smell of the new paint could not mask the aged aroma of the dark wood and moldings. Three certificates of some distinction, five framed art prints, and one black and white photograph all hung perfectly level. I recognized the art prints, and the people in the photograph were his parents. Giles looked exactly like his father.

"Let's go, Simone," whined Mia, longing to be outside. My eyes turned to her, and I placed the envelope in my backpack. Mia was struggling to open the door, so together we heaved it open. As it closed behind us, I heard the distant sound of the buzzer fading away.

Our morning routine was almost complete as we maneuvered along the now-bustling sidewalks. The crowds were slowing our journey, and we were now in jeopardy of being late. I hated to worry Father, especially when Mother was not home. We rushed down East Olivone and across Rue Predetone. Our city was breathing fully now.

I glanced at a street clock to confirm what I already suspected: we were running behind, and a shortcut was now in order. We wedged between a break in the buildings and from there followed an alley onto a quiet street. On Rue Treve, the landscape changed from storefronts and businesses to groomed townhomes, overflowing window boxes, and clusters of potted plants.

I surveyed the block and found everything in order, although I knew what was coming next. I could feel the eyes on me as soon as we stepped foot on the sidewalk, but there was no time to lose—we were late. Exactly seven seconds later, an elated girl with silky black pigtails and a linen dress leaped from a well-cared-for stoop and yelled, "Simone!" In her vault off the stoop, the euphoric girl toppled over a potted rose bush but gave it no mind.

"Good morning, V," I said in a low voice, while pulling the now-unbearably stiff collar away from my neck. Having a conversation with Gloria V. Cantone was like bracing yourself against a tornado, battering you with smiles, wide eyes, laughter, and questions—always more questions. I found it exhausting, but we had been friends for as long as I could remember. In fact, outside of my family, she was my only friend. "The V," as she was often referred to, was adopted as an infant into a family of privilege on Rue Treve. Our mothers described us as kindred spirits after we spent just one day of preschool together. She was always smartly dressed and, despite her rather petite frame, a hulking force of nature. The V was no shrinking violet.

Settling in about 25 centimeters from my face, she took one long breath and then her mouth erupted. "Didn't you get my text? I sent one to you last Friday. I was hoping to see a movie or maybe go shopping," the V said, with a hint of disappointment. "I need new shoes," she said. Pointing down at her feet, she immediately followed with, "Do these look old to you? I think they do. The colors have faded. Mom says I need new ones; these are getting worn. Do they look worn to you?" Her eyes quickly focused on my shoes. "Where did you get those? They're old, Simone. You need new shoes, too."

The V took a very short breath and continued to discuss shoes, which rambled into getting a haircut, the current state of her cat, Gustav Léon, and then back to shoes. All in under 30 seconds.

I was now standing frozen with my eyes squinting from the onslaught. The V was now seven centimeters from my face, but she paused.

Is something wrong? I thought.

With the posturing of a doting mother, she took a step back, and in a slowed voice said, "Gray again? You must have something colorful in your wardrobe? Gray is so, so blah!" She reached out to straighten my sleeve, which had curled up.

I sensed that the timing was right to enter the, thus far, one-sided conversation. "I'm sorry, V. I meant to text you back," I said as I nudged Gigi away from the broken flowerpot. "Maybe we can go see a movie this weekend," I added while straightening my glasses and readjusting my backpack.

Don't get me wrong: I was fond of the V, but doing normal kid stuff made me twitchy and I often shuddered in the wake of the V's frantic energy.

The V reared back and, with arms wide open, screamed, "Great! A movie. I'll check the paper to see what's playing. Something epic this time, not another cartoon," she said with a glance at Mia. Being slightly offended, Mia quickly stuck out her tongue. The V was settling in for a lengthy conversation when her mother stepped to the window.

"Gloria Veronica Cantone! It's almost time for your piano lesson." She then noticed us. "Oh, hello girls. Back from the park?"

"Yes, ma'am," we replied.

I glanced down at my watch and thought to myself, *10:48 on Tuesday. Madame Prissone will be here in 12 minutes.*

"Say hello to your parents for me," Mrs. Cantone added while walking away from the window.

The V's mouth chatted at high speed for another 20 seconds about literally nothing, and then she turned toward the stoop, nearly tripping over the smashed pot. "This is a problem. I'll have someone clean this up. Mom!" With that, she ran inside, leaving us panting softly.

Suddenly the front door flew open, and the V's head stuck out.

"Simone! When is your mom coming home?"

An approaching voice from within the house yelled, "V! Get in this house!"

"Later, gators," the V said with a wink while being pulled inside.

"We're going to be late," I said again to Mia with a growing sense of urgency. Mia grabbed a stick off the ground and pretended to twirl it like a majorette as we started off again. Only two more blocks to go.

We were jogging now as our journey was drawing to an end. Gigi was keeping up, although her stride was becoming labored. I picked her up and secured her in my arms. "What does this dog eat?" I said to myself, clutching her as she settled in under my arm.

Now running, we turned off Rue Dové and onto the first block of Rue Clodion. I checked my watch—less than a minute to spare! The sidewalk was packed with a line of people that spanned the block, and the aroma of pastries, sugar, and sweet chocolate filled the air. As always, this anxious line was leading to only one place: home.

7 Rue Clodion

L aFray's Patisserie is an institution. There is no other way that I can describe it. Founded in 1893 by my great-great-great-grandfather, Jean-Jacque Phillip LaFray, it is perhaps the most well-known patisserie in all of France, albeit one of the smallest. Some have described it as tiny, although I think it's perfectly fine the way it is, and *moving* is completely out of the question—it's our home. Every morning the specials are written on a faded chalkboard out front, and every evening the displays inside are sold out and bare. The façade is old and weathered, but in no way feeble. It is the kind of old that only six layers of paint, softened wood edges, and wavy leaded glass can produce. Above the storefront transom are painted black letters that simply read *Patisserie*. I helped repaint them four years ago, although they could use a touch-up. In the spring and summer, when the window boxes above are full and cascading, the letters are hardly visible at all. That's my favorite time of year. The name LaFray doesn't appear anywhere on the building, but why should it? Everyone knows exactly what it is.

While walking up to it always makes me smile, even after a trying day at school, the inside is my paradise. The wooden floors are dull and mellowed with paste wax, and a large worn spot sits like a carpet in front of the cash register. The front door is well-oiled and strikes a dented bell to announce your arrival. We reattach it often, as it has a propensity to fly off its hook. The display cases, which span the width of the store, are well lit and cool to the touch. The only other thing in the front of the store is a small round table with two wire-frame chairs, although Mia and I are the only ones to ever sit there. It is the best place to watch the customers line up. While the front of the store is organized and void of clutter, the rear kitchen is the exact opposite. In its center is a hulking wooden table piled with pans, trays, pots, and tall metal baskets overflowing with utensils. Only a fraction of the surface is usable, and a large pot rack teeters perilously above. The walls are lined with ovens, stoves, and cabinets, with recipe books piled everywhere. My father is quite possibly the finest chocolatier and pastry chef in France, although his kitchen would win no awards.

Speaking of our recipe books—they are legendary. There are a total of 73. One is solely devoted to chocolate turtles, and an entire set of five volumes contains nothing but recipes for fillings and icings. Each is well-worn, bound by an assortment of tapes and twine, and none have labels. Most of the recipes were handwritten by my great-great-great-grandfather himself with notes and drawings added on the edges by my grandfather and father. No one is allowed to read through them, and there are no copies.

To be honest, I have snuck downstairs and read through them countless times. Most people would see them as old, stained books, but to me they are family albums, full of memories and history. Since I was six, I could tell the handwriting and doodle marks of each inscriber. My grandfather, Michael Beresford LaFray, was the only lefty, but my great-grandfather, Thomas John LaFray, had a particularly heavy hand. It's unmistakable. These books and this store are perfect "as is." To me, the store is family, the store is safety, and most important of all, the store is where I'm a normal 12-year-old.

I'm proud to say that we are the fourth generation of the LaFrays to have lived on the sixth floor of 7 Rue Clodion, and we have no intention of leaving. Our apartment, which is connected to the patisserie via a narrow rear staircase, is uncluttered, organized, and decorated with a subdued tasteful touch. The walls and ceilings are all an aged white, and the floors are dark wood. The rooms are old but welcoming and calm. While the store is run by my father, Mother is in charge of the apartment. The four of us, or five when counting Gigi, are happy here; it's perfect. Many of our guests may describe it as cozy or maybe even cramped, although we all have separate bedrooms, and I have a small balcony that overlooks the lights of the district. I often count them just before dozing off to sleep.

The sidewalk was hot and crammed as we made our way down Rue Clodion. Mia led the way, of course, politely saying "Excuse us" or "Good morning" as we neared the store. I trailed behind, holding Gigi, who was reenergized by the crowd. Some of the customers recognized Mia; she relished the attention and pranced like a movie star walking the red carpet. I couldn't wait to get inside.

"Mia! Are lemon calissons on the menu today?" a well-dressed gentleman asked as he folded his newspaper over and adjusted his glasses. He was a regular customer and usually had his dog Archie with him, but not today.

"Mia! It's great to see you. Your dress is beautiful today," said an older lady with a short-brim hat. She had been a customer for years and only made it to the store on Tuesdays. She would carry a large canvas bag with "Produire" printed on the side. She would leave the store with it full. Mia nodded and blushed as she slowed her stride to soak in the attention. I think this was her favorite part of the day.

I could see the door. Red with "Bienvenue" painted on the glass insert, it was propped open by a steady line of customers. I was only a few meters away. I had left only two hours ago but was counting my steps to get inside. One quick glance up to see the flowers cascading down—it was exactly the way it was supposed to be. One last breath, and in we went.

Walking into our store in the late morning was an explosion to the senses. The overwhelming smell of sweet chocolate, candy, pastry, and cake was dizzying; excited customers clamoring to place orders, pots and pans clanking in the kitchen, a telephone ringing off the hook, and a tired clerk endlessly asking, "Who's next?" And there, beyond the displays and the sorting and boxing tables was my father, Louie LaFray. As if conducting an orchestra, he moved the many pieces of the kitchen in perfect, accelerated harmony. I could watch him all day. A rhythmic pattern of ovens closing, trays hitting cooling racks, and utensils clanging filled the room.

Mia pushed her way through the customers, ducked under the counter, and ran to the kitchen. "Father! We're home," she shouted as she knocked over a stack of empty cake boxes. I knew I would have to pick those up later.

"My girls!" Father yelled while stirring a bowl of thick batter. He dropped everything, wiped his hands, and lifted Mia into a bear hug. She always got to him first. Father was covered in flour, chocolate, and icing, but held her tight without hesitation.

"Father, this is one of my favorite dresses," said Mia as she dusted confectioners' sugar off her front. I was next, although my feet would remain on the floor. I have preferred to stay grounded since the first grade. Looking down, I was glazed with sugar, but I didn't mind—I was home.

"Father! You should have seen me in the park today. I was Little Red Riding Hood and Gigi—she was the big bad wolf," said Mia as she dusted the remaining patches of flour from her sweater. She gave me a sharp look, then turned back to Father. "It was my best performance to date, and all the parents clapped. Even Madame Preguet. She can be a hard nut to crack."

"Oh, that's great," Father replied. Mia was losing interest, as the front of the store was calling her. Gigi, exhausted from her morning, lay down to settle in for a nap.

"Simone, come talk to me," said Father as he walked back to his table and straightened his glasses. "How was your walk? I know you love to stroll through the city in the summer. Tell me about it," he said as he stuffed his hair back under his cap.

Conversation is not really my thing, especially when someone asks me *about* something. I could tell him in precise detail everything about the last several hours, but that's not what he wanted to hear. I paused for a second. "It was OK," I said as I tied my apron around my waist.

"Just OK? I heard today's performance was a huge success."

"I guess so. I was reading," I replied. "Oh. I placed your paperwork from Uncle Giles on the counter. He also said to remind you that he would be stopping by tomorrow at two," I added while sitting down to sort through the mail. There was always a pile on the desk.

"Paperwork," sighed Father. "Thank you, Simone. I'll look at it later." The bustle of the front washed over to remind us to get busy. Father grabbed his bowl and went back to work, and I focused on the pile of papers in front of me.

Opening the mail was one of my daily tasks, and I had been doing so for three years now. Nothing in the stack appeared out of the ordinary. The final parcel was a thick supply catalog. "Into the trash with you," I whispered. A loud crash came from behind me as a heap of cooling racks poured over the floor. "Not again," I muttered.

"Simone! Can you get those?" Father yelled.

Rolling the desk closed I replied, "Of course, Father." As I walked toward the front, I could not help but look at the customers, and—wait—*That's strange*, I thought. A man outside in a dark-colored business suit and hat was not moving with the line. It wasn't unusual to see someone peering in for a second or two, but this guy was lingering.

"Simone! The racks?" Father yelled out. I didn't realize that I had stopped to look at the man outside.

"Yes, the racks," I sheepishly offered.

When I turned, the man was gone. No longer at the window and not in the shop.

After cleaning up the mess, I dusted some pastries on the cooling racks, then went back to the kitchen to see what was coming out. My nose was telling me chocolates, maybe truffles or turtles, but definitely chocolate.

"Simone? Were there any letters from Mother?" Father asked me.

"Ah, no, none today," I replied, and it was truffles.

Mother was out of the country on assignment and would not be back for some time. When she was gone, she made it a point to write letters or send small care packages. Email was too impersonal for her, and she knew that I liked the postage. I cut most of them off and pasted them into my journal. Anything Middle Eastern or Russian were my most treasured. When we did get a letter, we would wait and read it aloud at dinner. Father kept all of them in a shoebox in the coat closet.

"Maybe we'll get one tomorrow," I said while trying to mentally recreate the face of the man outside, but I couldn't.

Father looked at me with a hint of disappointment but said, "All these need to go out front," while pointing at a mountain of truffles. "I think there are 32 orders there for afternoon pickup." I sighed and got to work.

After filling 29 boxes, I looked back at Father and yelled, "Do you have another rack on the way? I have three more orders to fill." He waved as if to say *yes* when my eye caught a glimmer of reflection from something in the pile of empty sugar bags. Father used the area under the table as a trash can of sorts during the day. By this time of day, it was usually bursting with accumulated bags of all types. The reflection was undeniable; something had fallen into the mess.

At the front of the store, I could see Mia greeting customers and making recommendations on their orders. Her finger would point into the displays saying things like, "Those are my favorites" or "You have to try these." She was the official store greeter, clerk's assistant, and customer relations officer. In fact, one Christmas, Father made up business cards for her that read, "Mia C. LaFray - President of Customer Relations, LaFray's Patisserie." All of them were handed out on the first day, which was no surprise to me.

As I moved toward the flash, I was sure that it was a piece of discarded tin foil or maybe a fallen spoon. It was curious. As I pushed away the discarded bags, I quickly realized that it was not a spoon; it was a letter. The envelope was undersized and covered in foil. On the back, above a wax seal, was embossed "International Federation of Chocolatiers, Paris, France." No street address. I quickly flipped it over and was mesmerized by the handwritten inscription that read:

> *Louie LaFray, Proprietor*
> *LaFray's Patisserie*
> *7 Rue Clodion 75015*
> *Paris, France*

I had never seen anything like it. A chill made its way up the back of my neck. I cut it open and pulled out a letter that was written in the same hand as the address. It said:

Monsieur LaFray,

We hope that this letter finds you well. The Board and Governors of the International Federation of Chocolatiers are once again pleased to extend an invitation to participate in the Chocolatiers' Ball, to be held on the evening of the third Saturday in August at the Grand Palais

Galerie and Ballroom. As you are aware, only five are deemed worthy to participate in this most prestigious event.

All invitees must confirm their intentions by the first Saturday in August. We are hopeful that your schedule will permit your attendance this year. Feature pieces will once again be auctioned to the highest bidder with all proceeds going to the French Benevoles. Should you give this invitation further consideration, the theme this year is Classic Opera. We optimistically await your response.

Yours truly,
Phillip St. Onge, President

Holding the invitation in the air in disbelief, I looked over at Father and asked, "What is this?"

He was sugar-dusting a rack of pastries and unloading something from an oven when he looked up. Unsure as to what I had said, he shrugged and went back to his work. In that same split second, his hand accidently hit down on a spoon, flinging it across the room.

I raised my voice. "It's an invitation, Father. To something called the Chocolatiers' Ball." I walked toward him, wiping flour off my chin.

He noticed me approaching and looked up. "Oh yes. Has it been five years already?"

My curiosity was now bubbling over as I knew my father's schedule better than anyone, and I had never heard mention of any Chocolatiers' Ball. "What is this, Father? What's this about?" I badgered him with a rising level of fascination. This was something new, and I had to know.

Father took a breath and started to wipe his hands on a towel. I was all ears. "The Chocolatiers' Ball is a formal event held every year. Five chocolatiers from around the world are invited to prepare a display of chocolate and sweets based on some theme."

A formal event? I thought. Sounded awful, but I needed to hear more.

He went on. "The displays are judged by some panel of fuddy-duddies, and each is then auctioned off for charity. If you decline to participate, you are off the list for at least five years," he added with a snobby tone to his voice.

Five years? I thought. This made more sense, as I had not been opening the mail that long.

Father went on further. "Simone, beyond raising money for charity, I don't see any point in it. Besides, why would I give up a perfectly good Saturday evening with my girls to go downtown and mingle with strangers? They are kind to extend the invitation, but it's not for me. Throw it in the trash, and I will let them know that I'm unavailable."

Without hesitation, Father went back to his work, and I placed the letter in the trash can. Now knowing what it was, I had little interest in it anymore. The thought of spending an evening in a dress, forced to talk with strangers, and—ugh, not for me. Besides, I trusted Father's opinion on this one; we didn't need it. As I turned for the cooling table, Mia ran by and grabbed the invitation out of the can.

"A ball! I want to go to a ball. Please, Father! Can we go? I could dress up like a princess," she interjected with heightened expectations.

Father smiled and said, "But you are my princess every day. Maybe when you're older."

That was exactly what I wanted him to say. Don't get me wrong: I love my sister, but she can't get everything she wants. Mia frowned and handed it back to me. In an instant, she was on to the next distraction. I studied the invitation again and admired its quality. The penmanship was exquisite, and I wanted to study it further.

Back of the desk for you; maybe I'll add you to my journal, I thought.

The rest of the day was like most others. The store closed precisely at 4:30. I swept up, singing quietly to myself, while Father meticulously cleaned the kitchen. He glanced up once, looking for the source of the music, but I quickly turned away to grab a dustpan. At 5:30, the trash was taken out and all lights turned off. The walk upstairs to the apartment lasted only a few seconds, but it was one of the best parts of the day. It was only Father and me. I had his complete attention, and the satisfaction of a hard day's work flowed over us like a security blanket. We talked about the daily specials, the store, but all talk of business ended as soon as we entered the apartment. It was exactly 52 steps from the store to the apartment and I coveted every single one.

We had our dinner, and then retired for the evening. I helped Mia brush her hair out after her shower, and I could tell that she was feeling the distance from Mother.

"She'll be home soon; don't worry," I said to her.

After tucking her in, I grabbed *The Count* from my backpack and walked out to my balcony. Becoming more interested in the movement and sounds of the evening, I could only read 42 pages. The summer moonlight layered a dull glaze over the city, and the lights looked like a sea of boats fogged in. "It's magic," I whispered to myself as I soon drifted off to sleep. That night I dreamt with ease, having no idea how my life was about to take an unfortunate and unavoidable turn.

The next morning was like most. Father was at the store early, but he returned to put breakfast on the table, as we emerged hazily from our bedrooms. After eggs, toast, and fresh-squeezed orange juice, we took turns in the bathroom and dressed for the day. Mia was particularly excited about another lemon-yellow dress, while I cobbled together a gray skirt and light brown top that would inspire no one.

By the time I exited the stairway into the kitchen, Mia and Gigi had taken their posts at the window, eyeing the assembling customers. About sixteen were crowded around the specials board, reminiscing about treats from their past. Mia loved to hear these stories and often reenacted them for Gigi. I cleaned the front window and display fronts and then started to assemble boxes. There was always a mountain to assemble, and the papercuts could be brutal. Nothing could be worse than starting your day with a papercut.

When this was done, it was off to the park. On our way out, we passed Monsieur John and Madame Tris reporting for work. They are a married couple and have been working at the store since I was a baby. They are kind and as much a part of the store as the ovens and pans. Madame Tris speaks three languages, which she often shares with me, and Monsieur John fancies himself a master chess player. He takes most lunch breaks in the shadow of the tower, playing with friends. I followed him often and played him numerous times, but I always let him win. "Someday," he would say to me with a wry smile, just after "checkmate!" It's OK; I liked spending time with him and found it more challenging to stir the match to a climactic end than simply to win. What's the fun in that?

As we passed them in the doorway, I noticed they were in deep conversation, but they mustered a dutiful, "*Au revoir.*"

Our morning in the park was uneventful, although I did finish *The Count*, and Mia's troupe apparently perfected *Little Red Riding Hood* by replacing the wolf with a fire-breathing alligator. Mia took credit for this rewrite all the way home.

The store was abuzz when we returned. Several specials, including lace cookies, cinnamon tarts, lemon cake, and coffee truffles, were on the chalkboard, to the delight of the mounting customers.

"Monsieur Louie!" shouted Tris. "We are almost out of lace

cookies and down to two lemon cakes." She looked over at John, who was carefully filling a small box with truffles, and said, "Why doesn't he hire another chocolatier or pastry chef? He works too hard, John. I am sure he could find someone." I overheard them banter as I was tying my apron and adjusting my cap.

With no discretion, John glanced at me and then peered at Tris. "Now, Tris. You have known that man for more than ten years. When has he ever opened his kitchen to someone else? Even Madame Julia is not welcomed in there. Are more raspberry truffles coming?"

Tris stared at him with a hint of a frown and turned. Now resigned to bypass John, she looked around him and yelled, "Monsieur Louie! We need more truffles!" At that moment, Father opened the back door and Uncle Giles walked in. I could read Tris' lips as she whispered to her husband, "Him again?" and then she turned to take the next order.

Crash! Another tray of overflowing cookies fell off a cooling rack. This happened a couple of times a day, much to the pleasure of the customers. Father had me display all fallen items on a "scratch & dent" tray out front. They were free, although we left a small collection box for donations to the poor. I had to change it several times a day.

"I'll get them," I said to Father, as he was halfheartedly working through a pile of paperwork with Uncle Giles. Father hated paperwork, but he did not allow it to darken his day. As I placed the damaged cookies onto a tray, I could not help but clue into the conversation they were having. Uncle Giles was emphatically pointing out fine print and pouring over a book of financial statements. Father longingly looked at his pans and gave me a wink.

In the next instant, the front door flung open and a tall, slender man in a chauffeur's uniform stepped in.

"Oh no, not today," I murmured to myself.

The man raised his voice. "Step aside, please. Make way," he said while pushing forward. The customers were bristling and giving awkward looks. The presence of this rather rude individual could only mean the arrival of one person, Sugars Fontaine. I had to get closer.

Standing in the doorway and surveying the most direct route to the counter was Florence B. Fontaine, or "Sugars" Fontaine, as she was widely known. Madame Fontaine was the president and primary stockholder of the Fontaine Candy Company, the largest confectionary company in Europe. One might delight in being recognized as the candy queen, but not her. She is, by all accounts, a horrible human being. Ruthless and cunning, she inherited the family business and grew it into an empire, buying out competitors and putting others out of business. The ministry had been watching her for years, but so far there had been no formal inquiries. As for me, I had not formed my professional opinion of her, although I found it ironic that such a miserable person brought so much joy into the world.

The customers were quiet, sensing that this was not a person to cross. "Louie LaFray!" Sugars yelled with a syrupy roll of the tongue. "You have not returned any of my phone calls. We have important business to discuss."

Seeing what was going on, Father stood up, excused himself from Giles, and walked to the front of the store. As he approached, Sugars' head darted about like a lizard, her face expressing contempt for all those squeezed into the store at that moment.

"I have been most busy. My apologies, but I'm not aware of what business we have," Father replied.

It was no secret that Madame Fontaine had been trying to buy our recipe books for more than 20 years. She was unwavering in her efforts, rude, and impatient. Monthly, her lawyers mailed one to three offers, which I would open and immediately discard into the trash. She personally came to the store several times a year. Each visit was more uncomfortable, and this one was shaping up to be a doozy.

She leaned forwarded and forced a smile. "Louie, we both know that your recipes would have a perfect home in my company." She looked up and drew her right hand over her head. "Think how many people could enjoy your treats." Her eyes studied the small store, and then the tone of her voice changed. "This shabby little store can't possibly be making you much money. You could be a rich man, Louie." She stared harder at Father, and I noticed Uncle Giles taking interest in their exchange. "Can we discuss terms?" she said with a hint of frustration.

"The recipes are not for sale," Father said as he casually wiped his hands.

Sugars' hands closed into fists on the counter. "Everything is for sale, Louie. Last month I offered you a king's ransom. I am losing patience, Louie," she said as her smile vanished and a look of anger washed over her face.

"I am sorry, Madame Fontaine, but the recipes are not for sale."

Sugars leaned in mere centimeters from Father's face as a burning sense of rage was now emanating from her body. Through her clenched teeth, she whispered, "Three million euros, Louie! That is my final offer," and she leaned back.

By now you could hear a pin drop. Every person in the store was riveted and hanging on each word. Where else could you find such drama at this time of day? I clutched my broom and stared at Father, awaiting his reply.

"They're not for sale," he said in a calm voice.

"Not for sale," I repeated to myself quietly.

It looked as if Sugars was going to go nuclear and clear the store, but something unexpected happened. She relaxed both hands, straightened upright, not blinking or moving her eyes from him, and smiled. Her driver was readying himself for a reaction of epic proportion, when Sugars calmly said, "You'll regret this, Monsieur LaFray. You will regret this."

She turned in disgust to find customers happily clearing a path. I studied her every step as she huffed out. As the door closed behind them, I exhaled in relief. I walked to the front of the store and gazed upon Sugars' enormous black and silver Rolls Royce, which had a license plate that read, 2SWEET.

"You have got to be kidding me," I said to myself.

My moment of calm was then interrupted as I noticed the same male figure from the day before standing across the street. Same dark suit, black bowler hat, and a shock of brilliant red hair falling from it.

Who is that? I thought, but at that same moment the store reignited into a flurry of orders and bustle. Arduously, I made my way out front, hoping to catch a glimpse of the stranger's face, but he was gone.

"Simone!" Father yelled from the back of the store. "We need these trays taken to the cooling racks."

I took one more look up and down the street and turned to go back inside as Sugars' car crept away.

When I got back to the kitchen, Father and Uncle Giles were wrapping up their business, and Giles meticulously placed the papers back into his briefcase.

"Hello, Simone," Uncle Giles said to me with deadpan delivery. He quickly turned to Father. "Three million euros, Louie?" he said in disbelief.

Father smiled and replied, "Now, what would we do with that?"

While the exchange with Sugars brought an uneasiness to the store, I could handle Madame Fontaine. It was the mystery man that I could not stop thinking about. Was it the same person? Coincidence? Was I being tested? Would he be back tomorrow?

All of these questions burned in my mind.

"This day just got a lot more interesting," I said to myself, but even I had no idea of what just happened.

Proteger les Gens

3

I awoke the next morning with the memories of Madame
Fontaine and the mysterious man fresh in my head. I rec-
reated the scenes over and over again, trying to recall all of the
important details. I only needed a shred, but there was simply
nothing there. The man was just out of focus, his face shaded, and
his clothing dark. Maybe approximate height and weight, but he
appeared to be of average build, and average is everywhere. Over
my oatmeal and sliced peaches, I detected Mia staring at me, waiting for the onset of a conversation.

"What's gotten into you, Simone?" she said to me in a frank
tone. "You seem all serious and stuff—even more than normal. Did
you have a bad dream or something?"

She would not understand the *something* that was occupying
most of my thought, but I had to say something. "Sorry. I guess I
miss Mom," I said.

With eyes barely open, Mia smiled and said, "I miss her too,
but she'll be home soon."

The moment passed, and sleepily Mia moved on and ate her
cereal. Twirling her spoon and almost nodding off into her bowl,
she perked up and said, "Oh, I almost forgot! I have to be at the
studio early, by nine o'clock. Madame Loy wants me there early.
I need to start working on new choreography for the summer
recital." She jumped out of her chair and twirled around. "I *have* to
be in the front line again."

"It's Thursday," I whispered to myself, with the day now looking up. A smile came over my face, as Thursday is my favorite day.

On Thursdays, Mia has ballet class for most of the day and I am given the day off from the store to train at the ministry. I typically went in with Mother, but Father agreed that I was now old enough to go alone. He liked to think that I was spending time in the library, visiting a museum, or exploring the city's landmarks, but that was not exactly the case.

After helping Father open the store, we left at precisely 8:35. We exploded out of the front door as Monsieur John was writing the daily specials. He was standing on a wooden crate so that he could reach every square centimeter of the chalkboard. "Some of my best work. Don't you think?" he said to us as we flew by. A small group was now reviewing the list, as he stroked on the final bits of flare.

"Looks great!" Mia shouted as we pushed through and made our way towards the corner bus stop.

Waiting on the bench at the end of Rue Clodion, I glanced over to spot the oncoming bus. Mia was a little fidgety in her pink leotard. I noticed that she had opened and closed her backpack four times already. Perhaps she was anxious about her day, or maybe she was missing Mother, but I needed to do something, so I casually put my arm around her and gave a little squeeze. She perked up and started to stand on her toes and twirl as she normally did. Less than a minute later, a bus with "Centre-ville no. 3" displayed on it slowed to a stop in front of us. I took a quick look back down the street and handed Mia her pass.

The ballet studio was only eight blocks away but connected by several busy streets. The bus was easier and certainly the safer way to travel. Mia used the time to continue her warm up and greet passengers, while I sat and opened my journal. I would sink into my seat and perform a warmup of my own. The ride today was like most others, six stops and fifteen minutes and eighteen seconds of drive time. I counted 72 passengers getting on and 58 getting off, almost exclusively men, only eight women. Typical. Our stop was next.

Mia was in a full sprint as the studio sign came into view. It was hard to keep up with her—she was little, but very fast. Her backpack was dragging behind and coming open. She had been a student of the Loy l'École de Danse since she could walk, and I have been attending long, overly produced recitals since. Mia beat me to the door, pried the large handle open, spun back, and yelled to me, "See you later, Simone." I was several steps behind but continued on to make sure she was received and safely inside. While I peered through the glass, Madame Loy gave me a quick wave.

I breathed a short sigh of relief, then looked at my watch; it was precisely 9:00. I had only fifteen minutes to get to the corner of Shafer and Rue Marin.

It was warm that day, so I pulled my hair back and started to walk with conviction. A girl my age would not run down the street—it might cause attention. The bus would take too long, so I decided to take it on foot. The exercise wouldn't hurt, and it gave me another chance to practice. I weaved through the jammed sidewalks without bumping into a soul or causing a second look. Humming to myself softly, I still could not shake the events of the prior day. I could recall the exact smell in the air, the color of the light pouring through the storefront, and the order placed at the precise moment Madame Fontaine entered the store. It was order #83, but still nothing on the mystery man.

I glanced at my watch again in stride. "I am going to make it," I whispered as my mind drifted again. In the next split second— *bang!*—I collided with a well-dressed gentleman walking in the opposite direction. I was mortified.

I blurted out, "Excuse me, I—I am sorry, my apologies."

The man was dusting himself and straightening his jacket. "Not to worry," he said. "It can happen to anyone, but please try to watch where you are going." And with that he stepped aside and continued on his way.

At that moment, I could not recall ever bumping into someone, much less almost knocking them down. I stood quiet for a moment, collected myself, and moved on. I was going to be late, and I was never late.

The next corner was Shafer and Rue Marin. At this corner was a newsstand of no particular note, although it had magazines and piles of newspapers in various languages. Several patrons were trading coins for reads with the proprietor. Behind a counter of sorts was a short, heavyset man with rolled shirt sleeves, glasses and an old tweed cap. Trading pleasantries with his patrons, he saw me and gave a casual wink.

I picked up an Italian newspaper and started to read it as the last patron moved on. "Good morning, Monsieur Leon," I said sheepishly.

"You're late," Leon said casually while closing his cashbox. "It's 9:16. Is everything all right?"

"Yes, fine. The sidewalks were very busy today, and I didn't want to wait for the bus."

"I see," he said as he restacked a pile of newspapers. To the untrained eye, this would appear to be like any newsstand in the city, but it was something much different. Monsieur Leon is a communications operative and perhaps the most informed person in Paris. Many within our organization do not trust electronic communications and prefer to have information handed to them directly. Leon was our most reliable operative, and anything you received from him was gospel. He would strategically place notes that looked like advertisements within the newspapers and magazines. These notes were coded and unrecognizable to anyone else. Mother was a frequent patron, and we stopped every Thursday morning before going in.

"They're waiting for you," Leon said in a low voice. "Move along."

With that, I returned the newspaper and started to walk. Exactly nineteen steps to a simple, somewhat shabby basement door. I looked back at Monsieur Leon, who was again helping customers. With his left hand, he pointed his ring and middle finger at the ground twice. I stared back at the door, gave two soft knocks, jiggled the knob once, and then gave a gentle kick. I heard the lock release, turned the knob, and stepped inside.

The vestibule was cool and well lit. A man sitting behind a small, wooden desk in front of me said, "Good morning, Simone. Please sign." He moved a ledger book across the table and handed me a pen. I had seen this man countless times, and rarely did he smile. I glanced at him, wrote my name, and slid it back. He checked the signature closely, looked at me again, and then said, "You may proceed."

I turned to the right, took four steps forward and was now standing in front of a metal door with no handle or peephole. It looked like a freezer door glued to the wall. Three seconds later, it opened, and I strode inside.

"Good morning, Simone. We have been waiting for you," said a reassuring voice as I straightened my shirt.

"Good morning, Madame Pilfrey," I replied. "I'm ready."

Eloise K. Pilfrey is a retired operative who now holds a special position in the ministry. Her official title is "Attaché to the Director," although she is the head of a small, covert division that is nameless. Mother told me she was born in France to a family of privilege but spent most of her childhood in England. She and Mother had been to every corner of the globe, many times together. Eloise and I had been meeting every Thursday for five years, and we had become close. She was my mentor, kind and generally patient, although she did find working with a twelve-year-old trying from time to time. She had one daughter, Claire, who had been in a boarding school since first grade. I had not seen her in years.

As the door sealed behind us, we entered another small room with a red door at the other side. Written above it in an old script was *Protéger les Gens*. I said it quietly under my breath as we approached it. Painted red with a dull brass knob, only a select few ever saw what was behind this door. Eloise grabbed the handle, turned to me, and said, "Are you ready?"

I nodded, took a shallow breath and whispered *"Protéger les Gens"* one more time. She pulled the door open, and we were greeted by the sounds of the busy office buzzing with noise and teeming with motion. The room was full of people swarming in an orderly fashion—some holding phones, some waving papers, and others intently watching their computer monitors. As chaotic as it appeared, everyone was focused and precise. As the door closed behind us, silence fell over the room and all eyes turned to me. This part always makes me uneasy.

We started to walk through the center of the room, as choruses of "Good morning, Mademoiselle LaFray," "It's good to see you, Simone," and "Simone, say hello to your mother for me," rained over me. I looked down, but gave a shallow, "Good morning, everyone."

A senior operative walked up to us. "Excuse me, Madame Pilfrey, but I must have a minute with Simone." He turned to me. "Mademoiselle LaFray, your theory on the Prague assignment was spot on. We broke the case two days ago. Who would have thought it—all those cats as decoys. Brilliant, Simone. Keep up the good work." He saluted us and melded back into the chaos. I couldn't wait to get into Eloise's office and shut the door.

Eloise's office was well lit, stark, and sterile. There were no personal items beyond one family picture taken years ago. Five framed watercolor prints hung on the walls, although these were issued by the ministry and held no special meaning to Eloise. I doubt that she had ever looked at them for more than a second. As the door shut behind us, Eloise turned to me and said, "I have some very interesting news for you."

I sat down, still trying to shed the spotlight of the outside room. I adjusted my pants, sat upright, and said, "Is it about Mother?" Eloise was the only person in the world who knew where Mother was at all times.

"No," Eloise answered while looking over some papers. She paused for a second and said, "We have it on good authority that *he* is here." Eloise sat behind her desk, made direct eye contact, and with a steady voice said, "We believe Reynard Baresi is in Paris."

I could not muster a sound, and my heart started to beat faster. Reynard Baresi, or "la Volpe Rossa" (the Red Fox) was the most well-known thief in the world. He was a virtual ghost, and some debated his actual existence. There were no known adult pictures to identify him by. After last year's incident, I pored over his file. As a school boy in a small village outside of Genoa, he was known for his vibrant red hair, which later helped to define his alias.

Wait—the man outside the park? Outside the store? The hair? I thought to myself. *Nah. It's a coincidence. He has no idea who I am. No one does,* I murmured.

"What's that, dear?" Eloise said.

"Oh, nothing. Just thinking," I replied

No one had seen la Volpe Rossa since his sixteenth birthday. He had eluded all cameras or identification for more than 20 years. This changed about a year previous, when he came face-to-face with one person: Mother. She did not get a photograph but was able to convey some details to an artist for composition. However, the ministry believed the description to be less than reliable given his use of make-up and disguise, but the hair—the hair was unmistakable.

"It can't be," I reassuringly said to myself.

Monsieur Baresi was by all measure a complex individual. He was not famous for the things he had stolen, and there were many. He was famous because he only stole what he professed to be "fakes" or "the work of frauds." The experts believed that he was once an artist who eventually became disenchanted with the art world. Monsieur Baresi would say that he was a liberator of the arts, although most would disagree. Ironically, nearly all of the pieces he stole turned out to be fakes. Misrepresentations of all kinds—paintings, sculptures, glassworks, photographs, and even jewelry.

Monsieur Baresi had committed heists all over the world, and they were legendary. After stealing the item, he would later return it in grand fashion. The item would be accompanied with evidence proving that it was indeed misrepresented. His deeds made curators, owners, and insurers of antiquities very nervous. Critics believed that he kept the original stolen works and sold them on the black market, while he returned a fake that he himself created with uncanny precision. Uncanny precision except for one, nearly unnoticeable flaw that would discredit it. I don't know if this was true, but it was certainly true that he was a thief, and he undoubtedly enjoyed every second of it.

Eloise opened a folder on the corner of her desk and began to read the contents to herself. I watched her lips move and knew exactly what was in the file. Eloise's eyes left the folder. "We believe that he has returned to steal *Blue No. 2*. It is on display at the Musée d'Orsay, with several other works by Jean-Patrice Claude. You may recall that your mother stopped him from stealing it. She stopped him exactly one year ago tomorrow."

I knew this story inside and out. In fact, I had been assigned to accompany Mother that morning in the gallery doing surveillance, but I'd had the mumps. Missing the action was far worse than having the mumps—they only last a week. The intelligence was spot on, and the trap was set. One small misstep, which still haunted Mother, allowed the Red Fox to slip through their hands and vanish into the city. Over the previous year, he had stolen and exposed items in San Francisco, Beijing, and Berlin, although it appeared his ego had brought him back to Paris. The male ego—so predictable.

"He won't be easy to find, Simone. We suspect that he has been surveying the gallery for the last few days. Agents have been posted, but nothing suspicious has been reported," Eloise said as she glanced back through her folder.

My mind was racing, recounting every detail Mother told me about that day. First, Jean-Patrice Claude was clouded in controversy. He was not only a painter, but later in life the teacher of several burgeoning students. Rumor was that an aging Monsieur Claude struggled with his work and took the unfinished works of his students, finished them, and signed them as his own. It was never proven, but it was strange that an aging artist, who struggled for years, was suddenly able to produce works of master quality. *Blue No. 2* was widely considered the masterpiece of his later work.

"Have you contacted Mother?" I asked.

"Of course. We're going to video link with her in a minute. She is busy but should be calling in any minute."

Less than two seconds later, her computer produced a soft chime and she turned it for both of us to see.

"Hello, ladies," said the familiar face. Mother's eyes tracked to me. "Ah, I see you got some rest, Simone. Good," she added.

Eloise straightened up. "I just briefed Simone on what is going on here. As we discussed, our intelligence is certain he is in Paris and intends on stealing *Blue No. 2*," Eloise said with a tone of authority.

"It's good to see you, Mother," I added.

41

Mother smiled at me and then brushed some dirt off her cheek.

"Simone," she said in a serious manner. "You are going to take a more active role on this one. I'll be here to support you as much as I can, but both Eloise and I agree that you bring a certain perspective to this matter. You are going to work the field this time."

I was not expecting that and temporarily stared at the screen with disbelief.

"The field?" I asked.

Eloise chimed in. "Yes, you weren't there when he tried to steal the painting. Therefore, he has no idea who you are or what you looked like.

She's right. The hair had to be a coincidence, I thought. I felt much better.

"Also, who would suspect a twelve-year-old girl as an operative?" Eloise paused. "You're ready, Simone," she said with a stern voice.

These were all excellent points, and I knew that they made perfect sense; but still, I had never been given a field assignment before. Rare feelings of anxiety and doubt bubbled up as I tried to remain composed. I had not experienced nerves for a long time, and the feelings made me uneasy. As I looked around the room, it was as if the walls were starting to close in.

Mother brushed some more dust off her chin and added, "You're ready, Simone, and you will have the full support of the ministry. No training today—it's time to go to work."

"I am ready," I whispered to my mother, and all doubts melted away. With complete confidence, I sat up, eager to hear more.

We discussed certain theories as to why he was back, but they all led back to his pride. "Well, I guess we are done here," injected Eloise.

Mother's eyes tracked to me again, and she said, "I'm here for you anytime, dear. You're ready." With that, the screen went blank.

Eloise put her computer away and turned to me.

"We have a car waiting for you. For the remainder of the day, you will survey Galleries 6, 9, and 11 at the Musée d'Orsay. They are the obvious targets, as works from Jean-Patrice Claude are in each of them. No other museum or gallery in the city is currently showing his works," she said. "Don't worry: we have agents roaming the museum should you need them. You will not be alone. If you spot him, send the message on your watch and they will be there immediately. You have nothing to fear."

I took a breath and quietly said, "Protect the People."

Blue No. 2

Musée d'Orsay was in the central district of the city, and it was my favorite museum. I had been there countless times with Mother and the family. It was always alive to me. Beyond the works of art, the salons lining the grand lobby were often filled with poets, musicians, and vocalists who filled the expanse with beauty and song. The building itself was magnificent. Permanent, inspiring, and grand, it watchfully overlooked the Seine like a king among the members of his court. The exhibitions rotated on a regular basis, but the core collection was among the finest in the world. Among other works, it housed some of the finest Impressionistic art, including several by Jean-Patrice Claude.

I entered the museum within a large group of students with their faces buried in touring brochures. They seemed like nice-enough kids, Austrian dialects and studious. I grabbed a program off an ornate display inside the vestibule and started to read it. As expected, the works of Jean-Patrice Claude were in Galleries 6, 9, and 11. Galleries 11 and 9 were on the third floor, while Gallery 6 was on the second floor. Moving through the museum, I started to take note of the people inside, the paintings on the walls, and the strategic placement of sculptures in the hallways. The familiarity within these walls was comforting.

Up the marble stairs and down the stoic hall, I moved along like any student and made eye contact with no one. I casually glanced at paintings but did not stop at any for more than ten seconds. When I walked into Gallery 11, there were eight people in the room—two men, three women, and three children. I eyed a bench in the middle of the room and took out a pad and pencil. To blend in, I began to sketch a large sculpture in front, as any art student would do. The figure looked like an assemblage of blobs with what appeared to be sticks or maybe trees coming out of the top.

I had been sitting there for exactly 43 minutes when an older lady peered over my shoulder and said, "That is excellent, dear. You are quite gifted." I looked up to acknowledge her, but the lady was starting to move on. I was vexed that she had noticed me, but she seemed harmless and sincere. I turned the page and started a new, less inspired sketch. I was in that room for a total of one hour. In that time, 38 people moved in and out of the hall without incident. No one looked at any of the four paintings of Jean-Patrice Claude for more than three minutes, and none of them appeared suspicious. It was time to move on.

Gallery 9 was only a couple of steps down the large hallway on the left. Upon entering it, I was immediately struck by its similarities to Gallery 11. The spacing of the paintings, the height in which they were displayed, the off-white wall color, the intensity of the lighting—all exactly the same in a mirror image. I again took a seat on a bench, pulled out my notebook and pencil, and started to sketch.

In the first seven minutes, fifteen people—eight men and seven women—moved in and out of the room. I tried to balance the effort toward my sketch with surveying of the room, but I was finding it increasingly difficult to do so. I was now square in front of a painting of cows grazing in a field. A master's work, it was good, but still nothing suspicious at all in the room.

I was starting to think that this was turning into a long afternoon of sketching when I saw something. A man leading a tour was hovering around an early painting of Jean-Patrice Claude, for three minutes and 37 seconds, to be precise. He was not wearing a museum uniform, and it was the only painting they were studying.

Although a masterwork, it was not considered one of his finer paintings. *Odd,* I thought.

From where I was seated, I could not fully observe the man, as he was moving back and forth in front of his group. On previous assignments, I would have been in a van outside or perhaps back at the command center, but this situation called for action. I was in the field this time, and I needed to interact in the situation. I had only practiced this type of thing in training exercises, but I had to try something. Doing my best to channel a chatty teenager, specifically the V, I walked right up to the man.

"Excuse me sir, but are you a tour guide? I love to take art tours. Are you giving another tour later today? Do you have a business card? Maybe my parents could buy me a ticket for my birthday or something. Did I mention that I love art?" The man paused and stared at me. Without a word, he reached into his pocket, pulled out a single card, and handed it over.

"I really have to get back to my group now," he said in a low voice as he turned his head and went on with his lecture. The man concluded his lecture and then ushered the group out of the room.

Portraying a tour guide was too obvious, but perhaps he was an accomplice or maybe a diversion. I slid the card across the face of my watch as it blinked. Six seconds later a message appeared that the man was in fact a private tour guide in Paris and had no criminal record. He checked out. I sat back down for twelve more minutes and counted an additional 23 people moving through the room, none suspicious. It was time to move on to Gallery 6.

Walking through the museum was like exploring a wonderland. Art and inspiration filled every glance, and the structure itself was magnificent. Large in scale, open, and permanent. On my way down a window-lined staircase, my eye caught the reflection of the building in the ripples of the Seine. Even though I was deep in thought, I could not help but take in the beauty around me. I love this city.

Walking into Gallery 6, I noticed a man in a light-colored suit leaning against the wall. He was reading a newspaper with his face blocked. *That agent needs more training*, I thought. I knew this agent, although he had only been in the field about one year. He was trying to blend in, but who would still be reading a newspaper that was a week old? I noticed it immediately. Who reads an old newspaper? I was particularly astute at picking out people who were purposely trying to blend in or appear unmemorable. In my experience, most people were trying to be seen in some manner, and few were simply fading into the walls. This agent was clearly doing the latter.

As I passed by him, I raised my right hand, extending my pointer finger fully and half of my middle finger, and appeared to brush something off my sweater. It transpired in less than three seconds, but it was visible to the agent. The man shuffled his paper, turned a page, and went back to reading. I signaled him so that he knew I was going in and to stay alert.

This gallery was much larger than the others and had multiple exhibitions from around the world. It was contemporary in finish, and the air was colder. Six degrees colder, to be exact. My eyes were immediately drawn to the far back corner, which displayed several later works of Jean-Patrice Claude. After a quick glance across the room, I strolled the perimeter, appearing to study the exhibitions. There was much to take in. Finally landing at minimalist works from mid-century China, I glanced over, and there on the wall, only twelve steps away, was *Blue No. 2*. I could feel my heart rate rising.

I had not seen the painting for several months, but it was beautiful. As I walked up, a man who had been staring at it noticed me and said, "A masterpiece. Don't you think?" The man took one last look and walked away. The painting was now all mine.

It measured about 86 centimeters by 72 centimeters and was

set in a gilded gold frame that was slightly understated. All of the works in this series used blue tones only, and all depicted specific times of one particular day. *Blue No. 2* captured dusk over a central France countryside that was stunning. Swirls and bold strokes covered the canvas, which gave it a dreamlike texture. I could stare at it for hours. Regaining my sense of purpose, I turned and sat on a backless marble bench. The tablet came back out, and I started to sketch.

In the first hour, 27 people came in and out of the room, and only two stopped at the painting. I was not looking for the obvious. Anyone could find the placement of the security cameras, the exits, the guards, the methods of display. I was looking for something else. I see the room and those in it within a sort of rhythmic dance. Something like a moving 3-D painting. Order, flow, patterns unfold, and I can read them perfectly. I was searching for the outlier, the one not moving in step, the one out of rhythm. Kind of like the agent in the hall. I'll have to say something to Eloise about that.

Another 17 minutes passed, and I was finishing my sixth sketch. I checked my watch to see if there was any news, but I knew time was running short. The flow of people was starting to pick up, as the afternoon tours were underway. There was only one clean page left in my tablet, and I was starting to get tired and a little hungry. I checked in my bag, but no snacks today. While blocking out my sketch, I noticed that a man sat on the opposite side of the bench facing the door. It was Agent Leon.

"Simone, you're not going to catch him today," he said in a whisper.

My eyes did not leave my tablet, and in a quiet voice I replied, "I am sorry, sir; I do not have the time." This was the proper response to give to a fellow agent, and I continued to sketch without missing a beat.

"Of course, my apologies," he said. His voiced trailed away as he walked toward the doorway. It was unprofessional, but he was right. We were not going to catch him today. A few minutes passed quickly, and it was time to go. I had only 30 minutes to pick up Mia. I made one last mental image of the room and collected my things.

Walking through the grand lobby was always a treat, even when exiting the building with a twinge of disappointment. It had a hum of excitement, and sometimes music flowed softly from the salons. Large groups of tourists moved about like a waddle of penguins chatting and pointing. Navigating around several of them, my ears were hooked by soft music cascading from the side. I took several steps to get closer. *Just for a second*, I thought. A vocalist was singing "Vissi d'arte," which was from one of my favorite operas. All thoughts faded as the music permeated my mind, and I started to hum along. My lips began to move, and my voice grew in harmony with the soloist.

The next thing I knew, a crowd of German tourists engulfed me. Twirling and trying not to lose my balance within the chaos, I bounced around like a pinball. Working the field would take some getting used to; this never happened to me in the van. The entire episode lasted eight seconds, and I came out the other end a bit miffed but unscathed.

I finally made my way outside and was greeted by the fresh, warm air and sounds of buses leaving the curb. Scurrying down the steps and trying not to jettison my backpack, I checked my watch. Only 23 minutes to get across town. It was going to be close. I almost jogged while crossing the plaza toward the bus stop. Halfway across, my eye caught sight of a woman wearing a yellow hat and oversized sunglasses. The figure was sitting on the transit bench taking photographs of pigeons and eating something out of a paper bag. It was Eloise, and she wanted something. I slowed, looked up and down the street, then casually walked over and sat down.

"Nice weather today," Eloise said in a rather pedestrian manner.

"Nothing, absolutely nothing," I responded.

"Ah, you're disappointed. You thought you were going to catch him red-handed, did you? Working the field takes patience, Simone," she said, continuing to snap pictures.

I looked back into my pack to see if there were any hidden snacks. I was really getting hungry. "Perhaps he's working with a team this time, or maybe your intelligence was wrong. I didn't see anything," I said as I looked down the street, hoping to spot the connecting bus.

"We thought of that, but we are certain that he's working alone," Eloise said under her breath.

I looked at my watch again. I was going to be late. "I need to get going," I whispered.

"We have a car waiting across the street for you. The dark blue sedan, third from the corner. The driver will get you there with time to spare," Eloise said, reloading her camera.

"Thank you," I said, while hoisting my backpack onto my shoulder and stepping away. Relieved, I turned and said, "Oh, your man in Gallery 6 was getting bored. I guess it was a long day."

Eloise looked away and said nothing.

As I walked away, I detected something shoved in the side pocket of my backpack. It formed something of a bulge, and I hoped that it was a pack of crackers. I pulled it out, but it wasn't crackers. My disappointment was quickly filled by curiosity. "What's this?" I murmured as I opened it.

It was a crisp piece of stationery that had been folded over twice. It simply read,

I see you, Simone.
Best regards,
- R

The warmth ran out of my face, and it was difficult to keep walking forward, but the door to the sedan was opening and I was running late. I tossed my backpack in and jumped onto the rigid back seat.

"Loy l'École de Danse," I said to the driver. He nodded and pulled us into traffic. We were there in a flash.

The car sped away, leaving me on the curb with a spinning head. As I paced in front of the building, the mob of unruly German tourists played through my head over and over again—it all happened too fast.

The front door of the studio burst open with miniature balle-rinas spilling out onto the sidewalk. From the center of the gaggle emerged Mia with her arms around two friends. "Simone! You should have seen me today! I was spectacular!" she yelled through a beaming smile.

I quickly readjusted to the role of a big sister and said, "You can tell me all about it later. We need to get going. Do you have all your things?" Her classmates stepped up for hugs and to say good-bye as I knelt down to check her backpack. Madame Loy stuck her head out and said, "Great job, Mia. Please come again early next time." Mia blushed, and we were off.

That evening, I sat on the balcony poring over every detail of the day. It was a perfect night, but even Paris seemed uninteresting in comparison to the day's events. I made notes, glanced back at the sketches, even diagramed the galleries and lobby, but could recall nothing significant or ignite any spark of detail. There was simply nothing. Long after midnight, I finally accepted the uneasy truth that the Red Fox passed only centimeters from me in that gang of tourists and slipped the note in my bag. While the fact that he passed right by me was concerning, it paled to something much greater—he knew exactly who I was.

The Rue Marin Theater

The clock rolled over to 6:00 a.m., and I could not stay in bed any longer. I had been studying the card for hours, and it gave me nothing. Morning light had filled my room, and the sounds of distant car horns passed through my open windows. After tying my robe and slipping on mismatched socks, I turned to my wardrobe. It was old and painted white, although the paint was in the process of slowly peeling off. Most of the inlays had fallen off, but the cedar lining was intact. It was my great-grandmother's, and I knew every centimeter of it. With the doors pulled open, I looked past a pile of shoes and a hat box to find a leather suitcase. The suitcase was old and shabby, but looks can be deceiving. After placing it on the bed, I flipped the two latches and opened it. I keep plain notebooks and my computer inside, as well as some other things I would rather not share with Mia. The computer was issued to me by the ministry. It is thin, black, and completely unmarked. The security pad can be rather tricky, and I have to be careful because the hard drive will melt immediately if the code is incorrect. After opening it, I entered the code: left pinky on the pad once, pointer twice, ring once, then hold the thumb until the computer turns on. The device was coming to life and "connecting" blinked on the screen. In thirteen seconds, it came into focus, and Eloise was staring back at me with a look of concern.

"Good morning, Simone. I have been waiting for you," she said.

"He knows who I am," I said.

"'Who knows you, dear? What are you talking about?"

I took a shallow breath and held the card up to the screen.

Eloise's eyes sharpened for a split second, and she looked down at her desk. "I see," she replied, opening a file in front of her.

"We have checked all of the tapes from yesterday several times, and no positive identifications can be made. The lobby was full of people that afternoon, and the mob that passed around you had been moving through the museum for over two hours. There were at least a dozen similar groups in the museum that day." She paused. "He must have been waiting for you to come downstairs, and then simply dissolved into one of them that was moving your way. We noticed on the tape that you stopped for a few seconds and were looking into one of the side salons. Did you see something?" she asked.

Eloise was not a fan of music in almost all forms. It would not make any sense to her that I had stopped to listen to an aria, so I simply replied, "I thought I saw a man with red hair, but it was clearly not him. Too short."

"I will say, it looked like you were in the eye of a storm for about five seconds. Being batted around, turned about, and then spit out the back. Are you OK?'

"I'm fine. He is not going back there. He was playing with us. Playing with me," I said with a growing level of confidence.

"You may be right about that. However, he is clearly in Paris to do something. That is certain. Touring the gallery where he was humiliated exactly one year ago does not appear to be a coincidence," Eloise said with a slight attempt at humor. Humor was not one of her strong points.

"The store is opening soon, and I need to start getting ready, madam. Fridays are very busy, and Father needs me. I have to go."

After returning the suitcase to the back of the wardrobe, I grabbed some clothes off the floor and called for Mia to wake up. Gigi nosed their door open and gave a wide yawn. I sighed and said, "Time for work."

It was indeed Friday, which was my least favorite day of the week. Fridays were always busy in the store, and there was no time to go to the park, see a movie, venture into the city, or even read. I often referred to them as "no-fun Fridays," which Father did not appreciate. It was by all accounts a workday, but it was home and the only place I wanted to be today.

This Friday started like most. The store was full of sweet smells, and Father had been hard at work for hours. The cooling racks were full. "Good morning, sleepyhead," he said, darting between ovens.

With my apron secured, I tied up my hair and tucked it under a hat. With cleaning supplies in hand, I made my way to the front of the store. Right on time, Monsieur John and Madame Tris came through the front door. They were in the midst of a disagreement, which was typical. Something about whether cats were smarter than dogs or the like. Seven minutes later, Mia and Gigi had taken their seats at the front window and were delighted to see that a sizable crowd had formed—many of the regulars, although a small tour van had just slid its door open.

"Good morning, Simone," Monsieur John said to me as he tied his apron and read over the daily specials. He was well dressed for a Friday, although he had no cologne or aftershave on. Father did not allow any employees to wear perfumes in the store. It competed with the goods. Each morning, Father wrote out the specials on a piece of paper and left it out on the counter. Monsieur John's first duty was posting them on the chalkboard out front, but he always took it to another level. His penmanship was excellent, and he always added embellishments and even illustrations to dramatic effect. The job should have taken a few minutes tops, but he was regularly out front for almost half an hour. Father didn't mind— the crowd loved it, and so did John.

"Ah yes, peppermint-infused truffles, chocolate and

marshmallow swirl, raspberry calissons, and lace cookies. What a perfect end to the week," Monsieur John said with a smile as he turned from the counter. Monsieur John liked to build some excitement, so he would walk to the front to look over the crowd. Like a bearer of some important proclamation, he would thrust the door open, walk out regally and say, "Make way please—much to do—make way," as he moved to the board with chalks in hand. The only moment of Monsieur John's day that rivaled this routine was when he could say "checkmate" in the shadow of the Eiffel Tower.

"How's it looking out there?" Father shouted to me from the kitchen. With broom and cloth in hand, I walked to the front and replied, "Busy. Monsieur John is putting the final touches on."

The store was now poised to open, like a racehorse waiting in the gate. Opening the store, even on a Friday, was exciting. The smell in the air was pure delight, and the displays were now overflowing. Behind the counter, stacks of empty boxes were awaiting orders, and Madame Tris had replaced the ticket roll with #1 waiting to be grabbed. It was time to open.

I washed my hands, took my spot behind the counter, and braced myself for the rush. Father walked by, wiping his hands, and then straightened his glasses. Mia was twirling like a ballerina for the crowd through the glass, and a proper line had formed.

Father turned to us and said, "Are we ready?"

With that he flipped the sign to read *Ouvert*, turned the door knob, and the store was open.

I would like to tell you that we were not busy that day, but I'd be lying. In fact, we were overwhelmed. At 9:49, a large tour bus arrived and unloaded onto the sidewalk. Our store was mostly frequented by locals, but several times a week, tourists would converge to see what all the buzz was about. Our patisserie had been featured in many newspapers, and once Father was even interviewed for *International Gourmet* magazine. I remember it clearly—it was the first day in autumn four years ago, and Gigi was just a puppy. She was tiny and biting at everything in the store. Father never stopped baking during the interview, and Gigi tugged endlessly at his pant legs. Two months later, the magazine professed us as Paris' best-kept secret and a must-see. It used to be, but after that article, the secret was out.

By late morning, I was busy shuffling trays and taking orders, but the rather normal tone was suddenly jolted when Father dropped an entire bowl of melted chocolate on the floor. The stainless bowl rang out like a gong. Little bits of chocolate were always flying about, but it was extremely rare for an entire bowl to hit the floor. While somewhat absentminded, my father was no klutz, and he never lost his concentration in the kitchen.

"Simone, can you help me clean this up?" he asked.

"Of course, Father, you keep baking," I said as if nothing had happened.

"Thank you, Simone. I don't know what I'd do without you."

I was a master of cleaning chocolate and practically anything that could be tossed in the store. I guess while technically messes, cleaning up chocolate and cookie dough was not unpleasant, although it could be a little sticky. The smell of the chocolate was unmistakable—milk chocolate infused with almond and raspberry. As I was addressing the matter with a handful of paper towels, a bark from Gigi turned my attention to the front. It was not unusual for Mia and Gigi to be in some kind of trouble, especially on Fridays when they were denied their walk and time in the park.

"I can't wait for her to be old enough to really help out around here," I murmured.

Gigi was not getting enough attention as Mia was posing for pictures with the tourists. Raindrops were starting to fall, and the front window was slowly glazing over. "Oh, these glasses," I groused to myself, as they had slid down my nose. I had gotten this pair only two months ago, just after my last pair was crushed in Tel Aviv. It couldn't be helped, but still the old pair fit my face much better than these. Pushing them back into place with my now-chocolate-covered hand, I saw a silhouette come into focus outside of the fogged glass. Holding a vibrant yellow umbrella, the man oddly had sunglasses on; the rest of the face was too blurred to distinguish, but the hair was unmistakable, a vibrant red.

"Sunglasses? That's him," I quietly said. "La Volpe Rossa." I sprung into action. "Father! I need to stretch my legs. I'll be back in a minute," I said, untying my apron and grabbing my galoshes.

Father looked up. "That's fine, dear, but please take Gigi. She hasn't had a walk all day."

My eyes flashed back to the front of the store to see the yellow umbrella on the move and Gigi at the door with her tail wagging. There was no time to argue.

"Every foxhunt needs a hound, I guess," I muttered.

"Do not engage him, Simone. Observe and report only!" erupted Eloise's voice from my watch.

"I know, I know," I replied. My hair was now soaked from the rain, and my glasses were fogged. The yellow umbrella should have been easy to follow, but the rain and haze made it difficult. We were now six blocks from the store, and several centimeters of water had collected in my boots. *I should have brought an umbrella*, I thought.

Gigi was enjoying the chase through the wet streets and barking more than normal. "Quiet, girl," I kept saying, although she yodeled on.

"Simone, dear, we have a car on the way, but it will be a few more minutes. Do not engage him. Observe and report only," Eloise added.

"He's turning north and starting to move faster. Hurry," I added, brushing wet hair off my face.

A passing taxi cab honked. It was moving at such a high speed that it sounded like a bugle. "The hunt's on now," I whispered with a smile.

We chased on, and it was now becoming apparent where he was going. He turned north on Rue Desaix, and there was no doubt now.

"He's headed for the tower," I muttered. "Of all the places in Paris." It was curious.

The umbrella was 25 meters in front of us when he stopped in a crowd. He turned right and walked abruptly toward a tourist kiosk.

What are you doing now? I thought as I wiped the rain from my glasses.

A voice came from behind me. "Where is he? We got here as soon as we could." Two plain-clothed agents from the ministry were standing behind me. They were familiar and had been in the field for years. In the next instant, my phone illuminated, and Eloise's voice chimed out, "Simone, let the agents take over. It's too dangerous."

She was right, although the gallop through the city had been exhilarating. "He's over there ..." I started to say, pointing at the kiosk, but I was alarmed to see that the umbrella was gone. I turned to the agents. "He was right there." I turned back around. "He was right—There he goes!" The yellow umbrella was back on the move and heading toward the elevators. "We might tree this fox after all," I said to them.

The agents ran after him, although it was difficult to follow in all the rain and haze. As we walked closer, I could see the sunny umbrella shining out of an elevator car with the agents in close pursuit.

"He has run out of hiding places now," added Eloise. "Our men are only one car behind."

The rain was stopping, but the haze was too thick to see the first platform from the ground. The elevators stopped, and I could make out the umbrella stepping out.

"No place to hide now," I whispered with great expectations.

In the haze, the tower stood like a large oak tree. I stared at the platform intently, searching for any hint of what was happening. "They have to have him by now," I whispered.

The anticipation was driving me crazy, and in the next instant, "They're coming back down," said Eloise in a deadpan delivery.

"Back down? Do they have him?" I feverishly replied, wiping the rain off my watch.

There was a long pause. "No, dear. It wasn't him," she replied.

As I stood in disbelief, the two agents walked up, one holding a slip of paper.

"We found the man with the yellow umbrella on the observation deck," one of the agents said, handing me the slip. "He said that a man in dark glasses and red hair offered him 25 euros to take his umbrella to the observation deck and hand this note to the first person that walked up to him. He works here at the tourist kiosk and was on break. His credentials check out," he added, closing his umbrella.

Our fox gave us the slip. The rain had stopped, and our fox hunt had turned into a wild goose chase.

Disappointed but now intrigued, I held the note up and opened it. It read,

Simone,
Not yet.
Best regards,
- R

The next instant, four liberally-sized raindrops splashed the note like a snare drum, and the ink melted off the page. "No evidence," I murmured.

The walk back to the store was much less stimulating, although the sun was now breaking through the clouds and Gigi was far more docile. In fact, she had lost her voice and was almost asleep walking behind me. I looked down at my watch—we had been gone 47 minutes.

As we entered the store, it was still bustling.

"Ah, you're back!" shouted Father from the kitchen. "Grab your apron—we have displays to fill." As I walked to the back, Father looked closer and said, "You look like a drowned rat. Go upstairs, and put on some dry clothes."

"Ah, ok. I'll be—" I started to say, but I was interrupted as Uncle Giles glided through the back door. He had a large file in one hand and a briefcase in the other. Father turned to him with his head slumped like a child at a playground who was just told "Time to go" by his parents. Discussing finances was among his least favorite things, which was compounded by being dragged away from his favorite thing.

"Simone? After you change, can you please finish icing these eclairs? Cousin Giles and I have a few things to discuss," Father asked, staring at the precision of his work.

"Of course, Father, I'll get right on it," I replied. I quick-changed and was back in the kitchen in a flash. My hair was still damp, so I just pulled it into a ponytail.

Of all the things to do in the store, icing was my favorite, followed by smashing hard candy and sugar-dusting pastries. Father always had a large pallet of fresh icing ready to go, eight to twelve colors at any time, some laced with pieces of salt or crystalized sugar to catch the light. And the taste—like sweet whipped butter that melts in your mouth. I love it. Midway through my first tray, I could hear Giles' voice over the ruckus of the front.

"Did you consider what we discussed last week? You are going to have to make some decisions soon," he said in a hasty voice. I could not hear Father's reply.

It was odd that Uncle Giles was here in the first place. He only came by on Tuesdays, and he was always very discreet and never discussed matters of business openly. "Of course, Giles. Come, let's go in the back office and talk," Father said as he put his arm around his cousin. After all, they were cousins, and Father knew this made his cousin shiver. As they walked away, Giles peered back at the room, looking embarrassed—and, unbeknownst to him, sporting two large dustings of flour on his back.

"He's not going to like that," I said to myself.

I had just finished another tray when Monsieur John noticed that they needed to be boxed. While most of our customers came through the door, we also boxed up orders for several local hotels and restaurants. A delivery man picked them up at 3:00 sharp every day. John emerged from the supply closet with a stack of unassembled boxes.

"Simone? Can you help me with these?" he asked.

Assembling boxes was among my least favorite chores, although it needed to be done.

Midway through my sixth box, Giles burst out of the office, stopped, and turned back with several papers clutched in his left hand. "You can't keep your head in the sand on this, Louie. What am I going to do with you?" He left the store in a huff as Father slowly emerged from the office. My mind was now overflowing with unrest: Baresi, my father, Cousin Giles, even Sugars Fontaine.

During my lunch break, I took a reenergized Gigi for a walk, hoping to sort some things out. My brain was wrestling between what I was observing on the walk and the roots of recent events.

Of them all, Father was heaviest on my mind. It was the first time I had ever worried about my father. He was always the same; confident, carefree, and steady, but something was different—something was changing.

I crossed another street, turned the corner, and for only an instant forgot where I was. I was simply walking now, not thinking, not trying to piece all of the fragments in my head together, not trying to find balance, but simply walking. It was as if the city was comforting me. Five more steps and I heard music coming out of an open door. I was back at the art gallery on Strate Street.

"Strate Street? How did I get over here?" I said to myself.

The front of the store was again littered with vibrant paintings. Gigi and I entered the store and the same woman was straightening paintings on the walls. The record player in the corner was floating the slightly crackled voice of Billie Holiday singing "Summertime" through the store. I knew the song by heart and started to hum as I casually flipped through canvases. Gigi was busy nosing through some discarded packing paper in the corner as I started singing quietly.

"Your voice—it's beautiful," said the shopkeeper as she appeared from behind me. I quickly stopped humming and turned toward a sculpture. I did not want to appear rude, so I asked, "What time does your store close?"

"Four o'clock today. I usually close at five, but I am going out tonight," the woman said with a growing sense of excitement. "Tonight I am going to the opera," she said, executing half a twirl.

I turned to gather Gigi, who was now nosing in some potted flowers, when I heard, "Simone! Is that you?" It could only be one person.

There in the doorway was the V.

"Of all the places I would not expect to see you," V said as she walked in holding an assortment of shopping bags. "This is one of my favorite shops. The art, the music, the flowers—isn't it great?" she added.

"Oh yes, it's great," I answered quietly.

"Are we going to the movies tomorrow? You promised that we would do something and it's already Friday. I guess it's kismet that you are here." V was starting to ramble.

"Hello, V. Is this your friend?" asked the shopkeeper.

"Yes, Madame Fran. This is Simone. We are old friends," V replied.

"Old friends. Why yes," Madame Fran said with a bit of a laugh.

"I'm surprised you even walked in here. Did Gigi get off of her leash?" V asked.

"No. We were on a walk and—" I started to say, but was cut off.

"She has been by the store before, and have you ever heard—" Madame Fran started to add.

"Well look at that. I really need to get back to the store," I said after peeking down at my watch. This exchange was becoming unnerving.

At the same time, the V was getting distracted by some paintings next to her and started to lose interest in the conversation. "I am sorry, what did you say?" she asked.

"I need to get back home. Ah, how about a movie tomorrow? Come by the store at ten," I said while turning my back to Madame Fran. I could not get out of there fast enough.

"Perfect!" exclaimed the V. "I'll see you then."

I really didn't want to go to the movies, but I did enjoy time with the V, and a little distraction couldn't hurt. In general, I find movies too predictable and overacted, but I do like popcorn and the solitude of the theater.

As we turned the corner, only a few puddles remained and the line was nearing the end of the block. I moved along with my head down and slipped through the front door with a group of tourists. At that time of day, and especially on Fridays, the store started to feel a little exhausted. By now, Father would be done in the kitchen and helping at the counter. Some of the tourists were trying to take pictures of him, but he found this distracting while filling orders. Regardless, he always smiled and made all feel welcome.

My apron was once again secure, and it was time to make the final push of the week. The delivery was ready right on time, and all the displays were sold out less than an hour before closing time. With the last customer exiting the store and the doorbell falling silent, I noticed Father step away from the counter and walk back to the kitchen desk. He walked with a sense of fatigue that I was not accustomed to seeing. He slumped into the chair and placed his face in his hands for a few seconds. He stood up and sluggishly made his way to the closet for cleaning supplies. Something was not right.

That evening, after tucking Mia in, I checked in with Eloise. Surely she had some news.

"Why would he come to your store? No, too reckless," she said.

"I would say the same thing, but that hair. It has to be him," I replied. "It could be coincidence, but the man outside made sure that I saw him. I'm sure of it."

"But you still cannot describe his face, dear." Eloise paused and looked over her screen at something. "Let's hold off making conclusions for now and move on," she added in a tone that signaled that this conversation was over. It seems to me that adults always want to "move on" when they are done with you. It's annoying, but we were getting nowhere.

The view of the city that night was somewhat somber, as an evening fog had moved in. Just after eleven, my watch began blinking. It was Mother.

Wherever she was, she was firmly planted in the middle of a deluge, holding an umbrella with conviction.

"Mother? Where are you?" I asked.

Pushing her soaked hair out of her face she said, "Not important, dear. Eloise tells me you had a visitor today."

"It was him, I know it was him."

"You're certain?" she replied.

"Yes, certain. No one else could hide in plain view like that to avoid being identified. He knew exactly where to stand and was gone in an instant. It had to be him."

Mother pushed her hair back again and wiped off her face. "It's him, Simone. I believe you spotted him, but that doesn't explain why he was there in the first place. He is a complex character and could be in Paris for any number of reasons." She paused. "You're doing great. Perhaps field work suits you." Her eyes quickly looked up, and she gave a wry smile. "Goodnight, Simone. Get some rest." And my watch went black.

As I settled back into my chair, the night sky appeared to be clearing and a growing sense of hope moved over me. "I knew it was him," I whispered to myself as I drifted off.

When my eyes opened the next morning with a start, "A movie with the V!" I shouted.

Spending the day with the V was like riding a log flume, running with the bulls, and being interrogated all at once. There was no doubt that the day would take several twists and turns, laced with a hint of fear and unending questions. Always another question. Don't get me wrong: I like the V—she's my best friend—but spending time with her can be a struggle. It's not that she is ever unkind or unfriendly. In fact, she is nothing but kind and gracious, but her energy and ease with others is the exact opposite of me. Unlike my sister, Mia, who would literally announce her entrance, the V left people asking, "Who is that?" by the way she dresses, walks, and talks. She doesn't seek attention—it simply comes to her.

The store was closed on Saturdays, and Father was taking Mia to the park for a children's play. She would undoubtedly try to make her way onstage, but that was for Father to contend with. I had the day off.

Minutes later, I could not help but notice the V's inquisitive face buzzing about the front window as she shouted, "Simone! Let's go!" I turned the key, and she bounded inside as if she was loading onto a roller coaster. Her pink and white sundress had been pressed earlier in the morning; the starch was still crisp, and her oversized black sunglasses barely stayed on her nose. "Are you ready?" she asked, surveying the displays for leftover cookies.

I braced myself as she took off her sunglasses and turned to me.

"Great news, the theater is running '40s classics all afternoon. They start in 15 minutes, and you know I like to get popcorn first. Don't you like their popcorn? Oh, that's right, you don't like it buttered. Salt only, right?"

It occurred to me that I was underdressed in my bland attire. "It will have to do," I muttered to myself, trying to hand press the wrinkles out of my pants. I wished that I had put on something nicer that morning, but there was no time now. I turned to the kitchen and said, "Bye, Father. V and I are going to a movie. I'll be back before five."

Father looked up, and his face lit up. "Of course, Simone. Hello, V," he shouted.

The V gave a quick wave to him as she grew impatient. She did not like to wait. With a final wave, we were out the door. The city was ours.

The Rue Marin Theater was beautiful in an old and almost regal way. The ticket booth was in the middle of the outside lobby, and ushers opened the door to each theater. Theater 2 contained

88 seats, and 16 people were already seated when we walked in—eight women, six girls, and two boys. I could not help myself, but before the second preview I had memorized which seats were occupied (by number) and by whom. I also overheard nine first names, counted the can lights in the ceiling and the pleats in the screen curtain and knew that the V had eaten 32 pieces of popcorn so far. Now 33.

"I can't wait for this to start. I've only seen it once before. Ah, yeah, only once, I think," the V said to me as the lights went down.

As I was about to buckle down to mull over recent events, I actually found myself enjoying the movie and a rather lengthy (but quiet) conversation with the V about our upcoming year at Trinity.

With her voice rising, the V said, "I told you she was a freak," just before being shushed by half the theater. It was a much-needed distraction that helped me to clear my mind all together. As "The End" rolled across the screen and the lights went up, we realized that it was still early, and a big city was outside the lobby doors.

"Let's go, Simone! Please!" the V said to me as she grabbed my hand. "Rue Raffet is only six blocks away. It's the coolest."

The 1200 block of Rue Raffet was the center of an emerging arts district that preferred the contemporary to the classics. You could only describe it as "artsy." The block was a collection of art galleries, record stores, and hipster cafés, although the sidewalks were the main attraction. They were cluttered with street performers, musicians, artists, and poets. We had been there three times before, and while I preferred to carefully dip my toe in the experience, the V cannonballed in.

It was time to have some fun. "OK. Let's go," I said, much to the V's delight, and we were off.

"Do you see that?" the V said as she ran toward a folk group wearing feather hats. "I've never seen anything quite like it. I have to ask them where they got those hats."

As she walked to interrogate the group, I was far more at ease along the edge. A young lady bumped into me from behind. "Oh, sorry," she said. "Would you like some marbled beads?" she asked, opening a canvas bag.

"Ah, no thank you," I replied.

For the next ten minutes, I followed the V and marveled at her. She was singing and dancing and even posed for a one-minute chalk portrait.

"That looks just like me!" I heard her say to the artist. The V was in her element and I could not stay in the shadows any longer.

"Time to jump in."

"Simone! Where have you been?" the V shouted at me over the street noise.

Not making direct eye contact I said, "I was getting a drink. All the popcorn made me thirsty." We were now staring at each other like two kids in a candy store holding five-euro bills. What to see next?

For the next 20 minutes, we darted in and out of galleries before settling into a vintage clothing store. The V tried on hats and then sunglasses out of a large basket, while I actually put on a pair of heeled shoes and wobbled around trying to find a mirror.

"You look like a baby horse," the V said, roaring with laughter.

Embarrassed, yes, but I did make it to the mirror. The shoes were not for me. While placing them back on the shelf, I heard something coming in from outside. By the time I got to the door, I knew exactly what it was. A street performer, only a few steps away, was playing a familiar song on her guitar. The guitar, covered in stickers, was slightly out of tune, but I looked past it. The music was casting a spell over me. My parents would play this record endlessly, often opening the windows to let the wind take it. As I walked closer, I started to hum, and all remaining thoughts of the Red Fox and Father faded. For the first time in a very long time, I was simply in the moment, living.

The performer turned to me and said, "Go ahead. Sing it if you know it."

A small crowd had gathered and I wanted to sing. I drew a breath and filled my lungs. This was it, I was going to do it. As the first note flew, I caught the V out of the corner of my eye staring— and I coughed into a sputtering mess.

The V lowered a new pair of sequined sunglasses down her nose and said, "Simone? What are you doing? Are you OK?"

I was so close this time.

As our bus squeaked to a stop on Rue Clodian, I peered down at my watch and noticed that it was only 4:00.

"Great day, Simone," the V said as we stepped onto the street. "Hey, it's early, do you wanna—" she started to say before I cut her off.

"That was fun, but there's something I have to do. Ah, I forgot all about it. No big deal. Maybe we'll go back next week," I quickly said.

Begrudgingly, the V called it a day and turned to walk home. She looked back briefly. "Call me later."

As soon as she turned the corner, I muttered to myself, "I've got to do this," and ran in the other direction as fast as I could.

The nearest metro entrance was two blocks away and I had little time. After I got through the turnstile and waded through the crowd, a train whizzed by. It was loud, dark, and perfect. I knew the subway like the back of my hand, but I was not getting on today. Beyond the waiting platforms were a series of maintenance tunnels and access alleys that few ever got to see. Mother often used them to move under the city without being noticed, but I found them useful for something else.

A minute later I had made my way to a small inspection platform. I could hear an oncoming train and seconds later it thundered by. *SWOOOOSH!* It was just me and two well-fed rats now. I took a deep breath and both of them stopped to see what I was going to do. With my eyes closed, I started to sing. I sang with all I had, with trains passing and shaking everything around me. I sang loudly and filled the tunnel. It was great. It was loud. It was me. I had to get it out. No Red Fox, no Eloise, no pastries to dust—just me.

As the last car on the yellow line train passed, my voice trailed off and the platform fell silent. The rats stared and then scurried away. "Tough crowd," I said.

Now you know my best-kept secret. It's just me, you, and the rats. Let's keep it that way.

I checked my watch and had only ten minutes to get home, and yes, the face was blinking. Somebody needed me.

The Fraud

For my family, Sunday mornings were spent at Saint Florence Church in Grenelle. It was the largest church in the district, and that was exactly how I liked it. I could fade into the congregation and use most of the time to hone my eavesdropping skills. You wouldn't believe what people say in church. That being said, I love this place—it's cavernous, and we have the best choir in Paris. I find it particularly comforting to *believe* and share my secrets in prayer, as some things are better off omitted from the confessional booth. Outside of the store, I spent much of my time avoiding associations and membership, but in the eleventh pew on the left, I was every bit a part of this congregation.

"Scoot over, Simone," Mia said with a slight whine. She also liked to position herself in the middle so she could make a scene while excusing herself.

Once a month, Father Rossi would deliver most of the service in Italian. I had been fluent for years, so this was a real treat. Late last night, I called Eloise, who conveyed that the Red Fox was expected to strike in the next 24 hours. The Musée d'Orsay was to be closed for the next two days for cleaning, and her intelligence picked up several suspicious individuals moving in and out of the galleries. It would be the perfect time for him to strike. However, I was unconvinced. This was too easy, too obvious, and especially un-foxlike. Eloise agreed with me, but regardless the gallery would continue to be under surveillance, and I would be sidelined until further notice.

As the homily concluded, my mind had assessed six plausible

ways in which he might strike the gallery, but I could not settle on any one.

"This collar is too stiff," I murmured, tugging it away with my fingers.

"Simone? Are you feeling OK?" Father whispered to me.

"Oh—ah yes, Father, a little tired," I quietly replied.

Mia was getting fidgety in the pew. 30 minutes without any attention was challenging her. This was the moment when she would excuse herself to go to the restroom, but take fifteen minutes to explore, or go down to the nursery. On cue, she started scooting down the pew and said, "Be right back. Have to go to the bathroom."

As the collection plates were being passed, I reset back into the moment and glanced at Father. His typical smile was gone, now overtaken by seriousness and worry. I had to say something. With some slight reservation and with a stiffening collar, I turned to him and asked, "Is everything OK?"

He turned his head, leaned over, and whispered, "I guess I am not hiding it well. Everything is fine; don't worry." He gave me a shallow hug and sat up to receive the collection plate.

As it passed to me, I placed our offertory in the plate and counted exactly €283.60 in visible money.

A good week, I thought. This was more than usual, but I had to guess at the loose change. I looked forward to counting the money, but reading the bulletin was my favorite part of the service. I read it as the plates made their way throughout the congregation. It took about two minutes if I spent the time to look at the pictures and advertisements.

"Only three spelling mistakes this week. Oh, and one incorrectly referenced date," I murmured. This was typical.

"I'm back!" announced Mia as she slid into the pew. She had only been gone for twelve minutes, so the nursery must have been light this week. "Is it almost over?" she whispered to me.

I knew we would walk out in 19 to 21 minutes given the number of people that day. Father Rossi was exactly 11 seconds into the communal blessing, and I counted eight Eucharistic ministers in the first four rows. I leaned over to Mia and whispered, "20 minutes."

Mia asked, "Are you sure?"

I nodded.

As we exited to shake hands with Father Rossi, the sun was hot and any breeze had stopped. My collar was making me miserable in the heat.

"It is good to see you, Simone," Father Rossi said as we shook hands.

I cracked a small smile and in my best Italian said, "*Avere una buona settimana.*"

Father Rossi smiled back and said, "Very good, very good. Your dialect is almost perfect. Just like home."

"*Grazie,*" I replied.

After church, we would typically go to Garcon's for brunch. It was only two blocks away, and the walk was particularly beautiful, down a cobblestone street lined with well-kept townhomes with a view of the tower in the distance. Our brunch ritual was one of Mother's favorites, but this time, we agreed to go home and make brunch for ourselves. Father would make most of it, while Mia would act as waitress and manager. I was given the responsibility of setting the table and performing all clean-up duties. It was fine with me.

As we exited the bus and made our way toward the store, I felt a greater sense of ease wash over me. I could always clear my head at home, and Sunday afternoons were quiet and lazy.

"I won!" Mia shouted out as she raced to the doorknob and grabbed it.

Father gave a smile and pulled out his keys. The door opened to the expected accompaniment of the bell, but something was very, very wrong. My eyes opened wide in disbelief as I adjusted my glasses and pulled that nasty collar away from my neck. The backdoor was wide open, several tables were turned, and papers were scattered about the floor. There was also something missing.

"No. It can't be. The recipes. They're gone," I uttered in complete disbelief.

A cold lightning bolt shot through my body. Not here. Who had done this? Why had this happened? A parade of frantic and incomplete thoughts thundered through my head.

Father picked up the phone and called the police. He calmly turned to us and said, "It's OK, girls, probably a random thing. The police will sort this out."

Mia started to cry, so I hugged her as Father talked to the police. "Don't worry, Mia. Everything is fine," I whispered. My mind started to regain focus, although I could not shake the feelings of helplessness and uncertainty.

Father hung up the phone, hugged us both, and said, "The police are on their way. We should wait for them outside."

I desperately wanted to inspect the scene, but I had no chance. Outside, Mia was glued to Father's leg, and I stood silent. I could not help but stare through the storefront to assess the situation. I had extensive experience with crime scenes, but I was struggling to separate this as *any* crime scene, and there was no way that Father was letting me in.

The police arrived minutes later with lights flashing. I had regained my poise and now had my arm around Mia. After a quick exchange of pleasantries, Father handed them the keys, and the two officers entered the store.

"I know these men. They are customers," I whispered to

Mia. They came to the store on Wednesday mornings between 10:15 and 10:30.

One of the officers took a quick look around and then went out the back door. The other officer opened the rear staircase to the apartment. I turned away and signaled Eloise on my watch, but the waiting was getting to me. I had to get inside.

"The place is secure, Louie, and there was no break-in to the apartment," one of the officers said as they emerged from the front door. "Could we ask you a few questions?"

I did my best to eavesdrop on their conversation. "The back-door lock was picked or something. No sign of forced entry. Also, the cash register was unopened, and none of your appliances or equipment appears to be missing," the other office added.

"My recipe books are gone," Father said with a sense of loss setting in.

"Recipe books? That's odd," the taller officer noted.

"Those books have been in my family for generations. You must find them." Father was starting to talk faster now.

"Of course, Monsieur LaFray, we will do everything we can. For now, go through your store to catalog all that's missing. Make a list, and call us when you feel it is complete. We'll get started immediately," said the taller officer as they turned to walk to their car.

One officer peered back at the building and took a long gaze. He then shouted, "You might want to erase the specials board. Kids must have scribbled on it."

It was typical for people to write things on the board over the weekend. In fact, one patron wrote "Free Cookies!" on the board several times last spring. Also, from time to time, neighborhood children would draw pictures on it. Monsieur John was not amused by these.

I walked over to wipe it clean, when I stopped cold. I stared at the board in utter disbelief. There in white chalk and block letters was the word "Fraud."

As I stood paralyzed, Father leaned out the front door and said, "I hope it's something original this time. Not another singing cookie or dancing cake."

I shook my head and said, "Oh, yes, a cookie," with a crack in my voice. I wiped it clean and moved quickly inside.

"La Volpe Rossa," I whispered.

As I walked through the front of the store, everything was different.

I don't recognize this place, I thought. My knees were weak and my mouth went dry. Desperately trying to focus, I felt as if all former memories and feelings of this place were draining away. There was no order, no reason, no explanation. With a blank face and slumped shoulders, I made my way to the window and sat. "It can't be," I whispered to myself.

While Father was on the phone in an attempt to contact Mother, I slipped upstairs to call in. "Connecting."

Then Eloise appeared on the screen. "We received word that there was an incident at your address," said Eloise with a heightened level of concern. I knew that they monitored certain addresses throughout the city, although I did not think 7 Rue Clodion was on the list. I sat silent. "What is going on, Simone? Please say something?" Eloise said, her voice starting to rise.

"It was him," I said.

"Who? What happened? Simone, you are starting to scare me," Eloise said as her voice cracked.

"The Red Fox. He took our recipes. He was in Paris for our recipes," I said in utter disbelief.

"Recipes? What? Are you certain? Why would he steal recipe books, and why yours? I am not following—you're not thinking straight. Perhaps I should come down there."

After a short pause I collected myself. "The specials board outside," I whispered, "it said 'Fraud.'"

The conversation went silent for several seconds. "I will brief your mother as soon as she hangs up with your father. Stay strong, Simone. I will be in touch." The suitcase went back in the wardrobe and I went across the hall to check on my sister.

"Are you OK?" I asked, peeking in the doorway.

"Yeah, I think so," said Mia. "Why would anybody want those old books? Couldn't they find some new ones instead?"

"I'm not sure, Mia. Maybe they didn't know how to make a suitable eclair?"

We both laughed and then went back downstairs to check on Father. Entering the kitchen, Mia saw Father talking on the telephone. In the next second, she realized that it was Mother on the line and wanted to talk to her.

"Father, can I talk to Mother? I miss her," Mia said with tears returning.

"I am sorry, Mia. We just hung up, but she said to tell you both that she misses you and that she will be home in about a week."

Father gave Mia a long hug and then glanced over at me to make sure I was OK. The room still felt foreign in every way, but I had to do something.

"Maybe you should take a look around," Father said to me with a wink. It was not common for Father to acknowledge my ability, as he wanted me to live the life of a normal child, but this was an extraordinary time. "Come on, Mia. Let's start making that list," he said as they left me alone. Time to go to work.

After scanning the room, I walked over to the back door, looked over it, and then went outside. I stared up, then down the alley once, and went back inside. It was all clear to me now. I knew exactly what had happened, and my collar was starting to soften.

Father and Mia were putting the kitchen back together. There were utensils scattered about, and most of the pots and pans covered the floor. It was a mess, but we worked diligently attempting to get a sense of normalcy back. As we finished, I could not help but absorb the loss of the books setting in on Father. He was visibly shaken, but trying to hold himself together. These were far more than simple recipes. These books were memories and family—irreplaceable.

For the rest of the afternoon, Father portrayed calmness and expressed optimism for the days ahead. He made his ingredient lists for the week and checked on us often. The police called right before dinner to say that they had assigned a detective to the case and that he would be in touch. Mia and Gigi were now well beyond the events of the day, gallivanting in last year's Halloween costumes. I was in my room working through every detail and connecting the pieces. The actual robbery had made sense, but there was one large, hanging detail that I could not reconcile: the motive. My father was no fraud. It was time to call Mother.

I closed the door and the suitcase was again on the bed. I placed my finger over the pad and punched in a code and the screen read "Connecting." Six second later, the gray morphed into color and the screen came to life.

"Simone. It's great to see you. How are you, dear?" Mother said.

With these words, the world made sense again. I savored the tone of her voice and looked over every centimeter of her face. For a second, I forgot why I called in the first place.

"You look tired again. Are you OK?" Mother asked.

"Yes, Mother, I'm OK. I have so much to tell you. You won't believe—" I said right before she cut me off.

"It's OK, Simone. You are all safe. There's nothing to be afraid of," Mother injected.

I had never been afraid in my life and paused for a second

to consider that maybe I was afraid. No.

"I am not afraid, Mother. I don't know why he did this. What was his motive? Why us? Why now?"

"Ah. You believe it was the Red Fox. Monsieur Baresi himself. Eloise told me that he was back in Paris, but why our patisserie? Be careful and don't rush to conclusions, Simone. There are certainly others who would stand to profit from those books. Why are you so sure?"

Surprised, I paused, as I had not considered anyone else to this point. I was convinced. Who else could it be? "I'm sure it was him. He passed me a note in the gallery, and he left another at the tower. He knows exactly who I am. Did Eloise tell you that?" I paused to gauge her reaction.

"She did, but that does not necessarily mean that he did this. What else did you see, Simone? Tell me about the break-in."

"The backdoor had been professionally picked, no scratches or force on the lock. The doorjamb had three new vinyl rub marks on the right side and two on the left, all less than 75 centimeters from the floor. Also, there were faint wheel marks on the floor that were slightly wider than our handcart. It took him three trips with a lined carrier. I guess he then made a mess, threw some papers around to make it appear amateur and frantic, but he was done in less than five minutes. Oh yes—he also had his car or maybe a small truck facing east. He must have bumped one of our trash cans as he was leaving." I took a breath.

"Well. It appears you have it all figured out. So what do you do next?" Mother asked me.

"I'm not sure. I guess we wait for what he does next. Why would he write 'Fraud'? It doesn't make sense. Father is no fraud. Why would he write that?" I asked with my voice speeding up.

"I'm not sure, Simone. Maybe he is trying to throw us off of why he is really here. It feels like a distraction to me. We need to stay alert."

"I was thinking the same thing, but why target us? This can't be about the painting," I said with growing angst.

Mother smiled. "We won't know tonight. It's getting late, and you need to rest." Mother paused and took a good look through the screen. With her smile growing she said, "I miss you, Simone. I'll be home soon. Still some loose ends here, but soon. Make sure you check in with Eloise tomorrow, and Simone—stay strong."

The computer screen returned to gray, and I whispered, "Good night."

After I brushed my teeth, my balcony was calling. The stars were out, and every light in the city was on. I was safe again, but something had changed. As I peered over the railing, the lights were not quite as bright and the city's hum was distant and muted. Something had indeed changed. Something had been taken from me, and I wanted it back.

The Pecan Truffle

I wiggled my toes to separate them from my moistening socks. The dew hung heavy on the lawn that morning. It was cooler, and the park was moving at half speed. In fact, my jacket was needed. I wished I had worn my duck shoes. Mia was now in the second act of *The Three Little Pigs*. Her troupe was attempting to incorporate a fourth pig into the story, a particularly stylish and bossy baby sister. You could guess who was both directing and starring in this adaptation.

As I sat on the bench, my mind was full of thoughts of Mother. Recent events had not escaped me, but this morning, Mother was front and center. I missed her eggs and toast for breakfast, the way her glasses hung on her nose as she read, and her ever-present ease. My mother had an elegance about her that I admired and envied at times. She was always in control, and it felt like my world was starting to spiral.

I could feel the morning running late, so I checked my watch, even though I was sure it was 9:42. To be honest, I sensed someone behind me and used the face as a mirror.

"Hello, Eloise," I said without turning.

"Good morning, Simone. I have news, and I thought it best to speak to you directly," she said. "Do you mind if I sit?"

I slid over without lowering my journal and cleared my mind.

"It is good to see you, Simone. How is your father holding up?" Eloise asked as she placed a bag on the ground and opened a newspaper.

She's never been concerned about Father in her life, I thought. But then again, how often are you robbed?

"Everything is normal at the store. Father is putting on a strong face, but I can tell he's on edge. What's the news?" I replied.

"Pleasantries were never your specialty, but it's good to see you." Eloise's voice returned to a less conciliatory tone. "The word is that the recipe books are being offered to a select group of buyers. One in Berlin, one in Moscow, one in New York, and one in Paris," she said frankly.

"Sugars Fontaine?" I muttered coldly.

"We don't know the names of the prospective buyers yet, but I would assume so," she replied.

I peeked over her paper to see Mia's production winding down. Gigi was running after a squirrel, and the air was heavier and getting warmer.

"Do you know when? When will they be sold?"

"We are not sure, but the Red Fox can't pass up the opportunity to show the world. He has started bidding wars before, but something is different this time. Do you believe he is doing this only for the money?" Eloise asked.

I never really considered the recipe books as valuable to others.

"No. It's not for the money. He wants to embarrass us. He wants revenge."

Eloise turned her paper, "Perhaps. Your mother did cause him a great deal of embarrassment. No one had ever caught him in the act. Maybe he is back for revenge, but people like him are always in it for the money."

"Maybe, but he will move quickly. We have less than two weeks. I am sure of that. Do we have any leads on where he might be?" I asked.

"Nothing, but I will check in with you later. Have to be going." After folding her paper and grabbing her bag, Eloise lifted off quickly and walked off across the lawn. She evaporated into the crowd in seconds.

"Come on, Mia; it's time to go!" I shouted.

On our way home, we were once again charged with dropping by LaFray's Comptable Services, but we didn't mind. We were only in Giles' office for a few minutes, and it helped Father out. Gigi, on the other hand, preferred to stay outside.

When we got to the office, the mail slot was freshly polished and the front window recently cleaned. It was as if the place had never changed. The fan was again creeping from side to side, and five business cards sat in the dish. I found something oddly comforting about Giles' office this week, perhaps because it never changed and, well, Giles was family.

"Good morning, girls," said the approaching voice. "Is your dog with you this week?" Uncle Giles said this every time.

"Yes, sir. She's outside," we said in unison.

Straightening his collar and in a voice of pretentious formality, Uncle Giles said, "I see. How is your father doing? It is terrible when someone steals your belongings, especially those with sentimental value. Those types of things simply cannot be replaced." He paused. "You know that they were my grandfather's as well. Sometimes I believe your father had forgotten that."

He handed over the large envelope, which was full this week. I discreetly moved my hands over it.

65 pieces of paper. That's a lot more than normal, I thought. I smiled at him and turned to leave.

"Girls—tell your father that I may be stopping by to see him tomorrow, 10:30 sharp. If he is out, have him sign these and leave them for me."

By all accounts, the remainder of the way home was uneventful and ordinary, just the way I liked it. We walked by the V's house and found her waving at us from an upstairs window, mouthing the words "Call me." The city was balanced again, and as we rounded the corner onto Rue Clodion, we were both pleased to see a line of about 30 people seemingly undeterred by recent events. Mia made her much-anticipated entrance, waving to patrons, saying "Hello," and even taking a picture with some tourists from England.

I moved discreetly behind her, but stopped at the special's board. The only item on the board: "Pecan Truffle."

"That's odd," I whispered to myself. Father typically had three items on the board, and pecan truffles were made almost every day. They were never a special.

The store had built to its typical midmorning hum, which was music to my ears. Orders were being placed, the cash register was ringing, and pots and pans were clanking in the background. The desk was piled with mail, and a dangling clipboard next to the phone was full of orders.

"Busy for a Monday, isn't it?" I said to Father.

He glanced up from a stove. "Yes, very. I suspect most wanted to see if we were still standing. Now where is that—" he said before his voice trailed off. He was more visible now with all the recipe books gone. The kitchen looked almost empty without them.

"Simone! Can you get these macaroons and put them in the display?" Father shouted, holding the tray in one hand and sorting through the refrigerator with the other.

As I filled the back of a display with warm macaroons, I noticed a man standing in front of the register holding an open chocolate box. I knew this man. Claude Dual had been coming into the store twice a week since I was a little. He often wore tracksuits, I believe in an effort to suggest that he prioritized fitness, although his shape would suggest otherwise. His face was troubled as he spoke to Monsieur John. Monsieur John was apparently flustered with this conversation.

"Monsieur LaFray! Could you please come up front?" Monsieur John directed to the back.

It was not unusual for Father to be called up front, typically by well-wishers or tourists who wanted to take a photograph, but this was different. Father glanced up, placed a rack of something into an oven, and walked forward.

"This looks odd," I murmured.

Approaching the counter, Father straightened his glasses and finished wiping off his hands. "Monsieur Dual. It is good to see you. What can I do for you?" he offered cheerfully.

Claude peered down, then scratched the left side of his face. He was clearly troubled by something, and my curiosity was peaking. The last macaroon went in the display, and I started to wipe off the counter. I was not going anywhere.

"Well, ah yes, it is good to see you, Monsieur LaFray." Monsieur Dual was very nervous, and sweat started to form on his brow. "Well, you see, I purchased this box of truffles, they are the special today, and—here, taste one for yourself."

He handed a truffle to Father, who immediately popped it into his mouth. His eyes widened, and you could see all the cheer drain from his face.

"They are salted," Father said quietly. He paused, stood up tall, and said, "My apologies, Monsieur Dual. Please take a box of anything you would like. On the house. My apologies again." He turned to the chocolate display, removed the pan of truffles, discarded them, and returned to his kitchen. As he passed me, I stood frozen, not believing what I had just witnessed.

A wave of doubt came over me. "A mistake, a simple mistake," I said to reassure myself while Monsieur Dual happily picked out an assortment of chocolates. This event was not lost on other customers as a hum of whispers grew. Their whispers created a foreign tone within the store, and the prior level of excitement vanished.

Father went back to work as if nothing had happened.

What is going on? I asked myself. Those unbalanced feelings had returned. I had to say something to Father and plucked up the courage. "Was everything all right with Mr. Dual? He looked—well, he looked upset."

Father glanced up and calmly said, "Nothing to worry about, dear. Probably mixed up some ingredients, that's all." And he kept on baking. This simple explanation was indeed what had happened, but I could only guess why. Father made pecan truffles by the dozen every day. How could he have added salt to the recipe?

Father gazed up from his pans and saw that I was troubled. He was not used to that. Putting his whisk down, he quickly made his way around the large table. The rest of the store went silent to me as he put his arms around me.

"Simone, we all make mistakes sometimes. It's OK. I'll tell you what: we can talk about this tonight. Maybe a long talk might make both of us feel better."

Perhaps Father did make mistakes from time to time, and maybe I was not there to witness them, but the idea that he was anything less than perfect was not sitting well. In fact, nothing was sitting well with me at that moment.

The remainder of the afternoon went on without any incidents. I constantly kept an eye on Father and surveyed the front of the store as I crawled through my daily duties, my mind still racing—and most upsetting was that I looked unhinged, exposed. The invisible girl was out in the open.

With all the dinner plates dried and put away, I looked forward to settling in to a book for the evening.

"Come and sit down, Simone. I want to talk to you about something," Father said from the living room. I was apprehensive, but took a seat on the oversized ottoman in front of him.

"You're not a kid anymore, and perhaps I should start to talk more freely with you," Father said. He sat upright and tried to collect his thoughts. He paused for a second and then asked, "You are happy, Simone, aren't you?"

The question struck me as odd, but I quickly replied, "Of course, Father. Of course I'm happy."

Father took a deep breath. "When your grandfather passed way, I took over the family business. I'd been working here my entire life, and it was the only place I ever wanted to be. He taught me everything, and I wanted to carry on his legacy and preserve the most respected patisserie in all of Paris." He paused and looked out the window. "I love cooking here just as much as I did when he was here, but—" He looked down and said, "It turns out that while I know my way around a kitchen, I'm not much of a businessman. At least that's what Cousin Giles keeps telling me. I'm a baker, a chocolatier, but I'm no businessman."

Of all the conversations I had thought we were going to have, this was not one of them. I looked closer and for the first time saw my father as something else. The man who made anything better with a hug, the man who always said the right thing, and the man who made the world safe, was just—a man after all. Strangely enough, calmness rushed over me as I was able to focus solely on him. It was time for me to listen as Father became increasingly uneasy. This was no time to be an analyst. This was the time to be his daughter.

After a minute, Father exhaled and settled more comfortably in his chair. "I always thought that a good business had a line out the door, happy customers, and empty displays at the end of the day, but we're barely getting by. If it wasn't for your mother working so hard, I don't know what we would do."

Father stood up and brushed his floppy hair out of his glasses. "Perhaps I should have sold the recipes to Madame Fontaine when I had the chance." He folded his paper over and looked me in the eyes. "I'm happy too," he said.

Before bedtime, I made a call to Eloise. We had not spoken since the park, but she had nothing to share. No new information, except that many of the works of Jean-Patrice Claude, including Blue No. 2, were being moved tomorrow to the Grand Palais Galerie. The move provided an opportune time for the Red Fox to strike, so they would be on high alert. The weight of the day was hanging on me now, and I needed to get to bed. I offered no insight into the matter and was still trying to accept Father as something less than perfect. Just before going to sleep, I took one final glance down the hall. As I expected, Father's bedroom door was half open, and the lights were on. It would be another long night.

With the midmorning sunlight pouring through the front window, I found myself staring at the customers to detect any unsatisfied looks. I was becoming obvious again, which made me uneasy. Father was preparing a particularly bold slate of specials this day to make an amends for yesterday's debacle. He had been in the kitchen since 3:00 a.m. preparing caramelized macaroons, mille-feuilles, and cream-filled pâte à choux. These were saved for holidays and other special occasions only, but he felt that the community needed to be reminded of how great the patisserie could be. His confidence was back, and I loved it.

"Simone? Simone!" Monsieur John said to me. "Are you daydreaming? Please move these empty sheets to the back."

"Oh yes, sorry. I guess I'm a little tired today," I replied sheepishly. In fact, I was a little embarrassed. The broom went in the corner, and I grabbed the cooling sheets. My focus was at the back of the store, where Father was finishing with Uncle Giles.

"I guess that will do it, Giles. Same time next week?" Louie said.

Giles studied over the paperwork one last time. "I believe we are in order for another two weeks. Make sure you keep all of your receipts and all accounts until then." He placed the papers back in his briefcase as Father went in the storage room for more supplies.

"Good morning, Simone. How are you?" Uncle Giles said to me with absolutely no calculable feeling. He looked over my shoulder. "It would appear that there are more racks for you to return." He pointed to the front, where Monsieur John had placed eight empty racks on a counter.

"Yes, sir," I replied courteously. Walking toward the front of the store, I found a renewed sense of confidence. The customers looked pleased, Father was happy, and Uncle Giles would be leaving soon. Things were looking up. I proceeded back to the kitchen with arms full, blowing hair out of my face. The back door closed, and Father reemerged from the pantry.

"Did Giles take his box of macaroons?" Father asked me.

"I don't know, but there is a box on your table," I replied.

"I guess he was in a hurry and forgot. Oh well; place them on the sample plate out front. The customers will like that," he said with a smile.

It was almost lunchtime, and the store was getting busier by the minute. There was a proper line down the street, and the phone was ringing nonstop. Word had spread of the daily specials, and the patrons were more than happy to make the trip. Out front, Gigi tipped over a dish of gumballs, and Mia tried to collect them amongst the customers. She was having little success.

"Simone! Can you help me?" she yelled.

I was furiously dusting powdered sugar over lemon calissons and had accumulated a thin film of sugar over most of my body. I set the duster to the side and made my way up front. On hands and knees, I was weaving through the customers with fine-tuned precision when the door opened with a bang. The *Open* sign was jettisoned from its hook, and all the customers turned. I looked up in some disbelief.

"What is she doing here?" I muttered.

'Make way, make way,' said the well-dressed driver. "Madame Fontaine has many appointments to keep today. You must make way." The room let out a collective sigh, and an unmistakable figure once again stood in the doorframe. The liberally perfumed figure entered the store with eyes forward. She marched up to the counter, and with complete indifference to any inconvenience she was causing said, "I am here to speak to Louie LaFray. Please get him immediately."

Monsieur John, who was unimpressed, asked, "Do you have an appointment, madam?"

I had to smirk.

Madame Fontaine had taken a casual glance at the displays, but upon hearing John's response snapped back to attention. "Appointment! No, I don't have an appointment—now get him at once," she barked.

Mia watched the exchange with wide eyes, while I remained out of harm's way on the floor. Monsieur John was not one for rudeness, but we would overlook it this one time.

Both continued to look at each other, and an awkward silence set in. "And whom should I say wishes to speak with him?" Monsieur John asked.

Sugars' face turned a frightening shade of red, and her eyes bulged as the standoff reached a boiling point. Then a calm voice from the back said, "Madame Fontaine. To what do we owe this pleasure?" Father stood there, stirring a bowl of cooling chocolate.

Sugars' eyes moved away from Monsieur John, and her face relaxed. "I heard that you came upon some misfortune recently." She glanced over the store as if searching for something. "What a shame," she said before a short pause. "I would be certain that a master of your caliber could simply rewrite your recipes? At least one would assume."

Everyone in the store was transfixed on this exchange. It was mesmerizing.

"Why are you here, Madame Fontaine?" Father asked.

"I am here to offer you one last opportunity to sell me your recipes. You can write them down or perhaps type them if you prefer. It doesn't matter to me." Sugars was becoming impatient and looked at her phone.

I took in every word and nuance of her body language. She was clearly agitated, and her emotions were authentic. Pushing my glasses back up my nose I thought, *Perhaps the Red Fox is asking too much? Or maybe it's someone completely different. Maybe Mother is right?*

"This is the last time, Monsieur LaFray. Sell me your recipes," Sugars said, her voice rising and cracking.

Father paused for a second, glanced over at Mia, who was now chewing several of the errant gumballs, paused again, and calmly said, "I'll think about it."

Every eye in the store immediately tracked to Father, and silence abounded. Now rising slowly from the floor in complete disbelief, I felt as if a complete stranger was standing behind the counter. My stomach was nauseous, and all my fingers went numb. Of all the responses that Father could have made, this one was simply inconceivable.

Stunned, a smile widened across Sugars' face. "That's a good boy. You're coming to your senses." The customers started to whisper to one another, and a chaotic hum came over the store. Sugars' eyes started to wander around the displays again when she settled on one particular item. "Is that mille-feuilles? I love mille-feuilles! May I try some?" she asked.

"Of course, madam. These just came off the cooling rack. They are very fresh," Father said, pointing to the treats. He opened the display, cut a piece, placed it on a piece of parchment, and handed it to her. She took it as if it were the only gift on Christmas morning and put the entire piece in her mouth.

Sugars' look of joy disappeared instantly. She spit it back on the paper and shouted, "Ugh! This tastes like a salted sponge!" She grabbed several napkins and wiped her tongue. "If this is your special, Monsieur LaFray, your patisserie is doomed. Consider my offer retracted and void. You are a fraud, Monsieur LaFray! A fraud!"

My heart sank. Could it be true? Was my father a fraud?

An exasperated Sugars Fontaine stormed out. Several of the customers started to taste their purchases, and many faces soured. A stir broke out as many demanded their money be returned, and others simply walked out. I watched in utter disbelief as everything stable in my life fell apart. Within five minutes, the store was empty, the displays were nearly full, and the bell was silent. I did not know this place.

Several hours later, the *Closed* sign had been turned, the store cleaned, and all employees were gone. Father sat at his desk, staring forward. He had no expression to read, and his hands were folded. I stood in the corner, reeling inside. Everything had changed, and what would tomorrow bring? I needed to talk to him but could not summon the words. Nothing seemed right. I could only stand and stare, but after a few minutes I had to say something.

"Father? Are you all right?" I asked, walking toward him with a stool.

"Quite an exciting day, wasn't it?" he replied, straightening his sleeves. "I still don't understand what happened. I have been making these recipes for years. I thought I could do them in my sleep." He paused. "Apparently I was wrong." What remaining confidence he had started to fade away.

"Maybe you need a good night's sleep. Tomorrow will be a new day. We will be fine. You'll see," I said with forced optimism.

"I hope you're right, Simone." He paused. "I don't know. I just don't know," he added.

Father's eyes trailed off, then unexpectedly opened wide. He sat up straight and laughed, and a smile roared over his face. "That's it!" he yelled. I sat back, startled by this reaction. I had not seen him this animated since the national team won the cup three years ago.

Father jumped to his feet and began to feverishly search through drawers and stacks of paper. A tornado of papers swirled into the air. "Where is it? I know it's here. You kept it, didn't you?" He was working himself into a frenzy. "Ah. Hah, there it is!" He pulled the shiny envelope out from under a pile of papers and stared at its every detail.

He said, "I can do it. I know I can. I can make this all go away." He flipped the paper toward me with an outstretched arm and asked, "Will you go to the ball with me?"

The Dress

Father closed the store that week to prepare for the Chocolatiers' Ball. There was much to do. Upon receiving the phone call, the Federation of Chocolatiers were both shocked and delighted to accept our response. Father called exactly one hour before the deadline that would have forfeited our spot. In fact, they had already struck through his name and had two alternates waiting on speed dial. The LaFray family had passed on the event since its inception, but this year was different. We had only five days to prepare for what could define our family's future. Much like an opera, it was either going to be a cataclysmic tragedy or a resounding triumph. I must admit that the odds were right down the middle.

Father and I were in the kitchen before sunrise the next day cleaning and taking stock of ingredients. Father peered up from over a bag of sugar and said, "Simone? You know a lot about music. What do you know about the opera, *Carmen*?"

My heart fluttered as I stopped running the water over the soapy pans and grabbed a towel. I love operas and *Carmen* was one of my favorites. My mind immediately recalled an evening at the St. Ide Theater with Mother when I was nine. Nine and five months, to be exact. Everything about that evening—the set, the costumes, the score, the voices—was perfect, a masterpiece.

"Everything! Why do you ask?"

Father was darting across the kitchen, organizing and studying labels. He stopped for a second and said, "The theme this year is opera, and *Carmen* was assigned to me. I have to create a

Carmen-inspired vignette of chocolate." His eyes bounced from label to label like ping-pong balls. "And it's going to be magnificent. Do we have a measuring tape? I know we have one somewhere." He went on banging about as my level of excitement elevated. "*Carmen*," I muttered with a smile.

The injection of *Carmen* was exciting, although the accusation of Madame Fontaine and the specials board still rang like a gong in my head—was Father a fraud? I stared at him for a minute. He was confident and flowed through the kitchen with precision, but the evidence was mounting, and my mind kept arriving at the same conclusion.

It just can't be, I said to myself as I admired his every move. This was the man I knew. Regardless of the evidence, I could not discount the smell that welcomed me in the store every day, the joy from watching him work, and the endless number of perfect sweets I had eaten over the years. Surely reading from a recipe book alone could not produce such perfection? Or could it?

It doesn't matter at this point, I said to myself. *What matters now is moving forward.* "Father! How can I help?" I shouted to him.

Father paused for a second as he finalized his ingredient stock. "Tell me about the play, dear. What's it really about? Not the fluffy stuff," he added.

"It's about passion, tragedy, and stirring music. Mother took me to watch it at the St. Ide Theater three years ago, and I have watched it on television several times since." I paused for a second as a smile crept over my face. "Passion; your entry needs to show your passion."

He can do it, I thought, but my joy was short-lived as my watch began flashing. Father noticed it, too.

"I see that you're needed. Let me know if it's your mother. I have something to ask her," Father said, returning to his work.

My room was stuffy, and I needed to open the windows. Gigi

was nosing for something under my bed, so I stepped over her on my way to the balcony.

The screen on my watch came to life and Eloise's face appeared. "How is your father? I heard he will be attending a certain event Saturday night," she said.

"Yes, we'll be at the Chocolatiers' Ball Saturday night," I replied.

"'We'? Are you going?" replied Eloise with a certain amount of surprise.

"Yes, he needs my help. I have to go."

"I see." Eloise paused to think. "This is opportune, Simone. We have it on good authority that the Red Fox himself will be there trying to broker your recipes, and a certain painting is already hanging in the room. Blue No. 2 and every major chocolate producer in the world will be there. He can't help himself."

This made perfect sense. "Yes, it's brash and bold. He'll try and expose Father in front of his entire community, won't he?"

"He might, but we certainly will not let that happen," Eloise added.

My mind raced over the possibilities, but then a question blurted through. "Eloise? Do you believe he's behind all of this? Do you think this was all an elaborate plan to get my father to the ball?"

"That occurred to me as well, but there is something missing here," Eloise retorted. "Your father is no fraud. He is a great man. Fraud? Pah. Nothing could be further from the truth," she added confidently.

"I hope you're right," I whispered as Gigi pushed her way through the doors and onto the balcony.

Eloise moved some papers aside, and her work tone returned. "Simone, we need you to come in this afternoon. There is some pressing business that is better said face to face. Can you come in at 2:00?"

"I think so, yes. I'll see you then."

With Gigi now on my lap, I gazed out over the city. It was cooler that afternoon, and humidity collected in the air. Maybe a storm was moving in. *Another 45 minutes and it will be raining*, I thought. I felt Gigi's ears and rubbed her back as she settled in for a short nap. "I hope you're right, Eloise," I muttered to myself.

With umbrella in hand, I made my way down the winding staircase. Gigi, now pouting from her short-lived nap, stayed at the top of the stairs and watched my entire descent. Father was in full swing now as I grabbed my backpack.

"Father. Eloise is meeting me at the Musée d'Orsay. It's business; nothing scary. I'll be back by 5:00."

Father glanced up briefly and said, "Duty calls, huh? If she asks, tell her that I'm fine and not to worry. We are back on our feet now," he said. "But be careful, and make sure you are back by 5:00. I should be ready to go over design ideas with you by then. Yes, be home by 5:00 and, oh, take an umbrella. It looks like rain."

I held up my umbrella and smiled as I dashed out the front.

Even the grayness of the day could not tarnish the view as our bus moved over the Pont de Grenelle. There was something ceremonious about crossing the Seine that never tired for me. East to west or west to east, it was inspiring no matter what was filling my mind. Halfway over, I had already cataloged the passengers, and rain started to fall. For the next two stops it was twelve on, eight off, and then seven on, eleven off. My stop was next.

"Are you sure this is him?" I asked, flipping through surveillance pictures.

Eloise sat upright at her desk, mulling over a wide range of possibilities. "We are not sure. We believe so, but these pictures are inconclusive."

Every detail of the photographs—the galleries, the people, the shadows, the paintings on the walls—sifted through my brain. It was all coming to life. I could feel it.

"They were taken in the three days before *Blue No. 2* was sealed and moved to the Grand Palais," Eloise said while pointing at the photos. "You can see that a man of similar size walked up and studied the painting extensively each day for about two minutes. A different hat each day to hide the face. He wears it in and out of the gallery. It never comes off."

I looked at the time and date stamps and compared the movement of the figure through the building. *Something is sticking out; something is not right,* I thought as I feverishly flipped through images. Something was out of balance; there was an outlier.

"That's not him," I stated.

Eloise stopped fidgeting with her pen and stared at me. "Are you sure? We were certain."

"That's not him." I said as my finger moved across the photograph to another. "That's him."

Eloise took the picture and squinted at the lower left-hand corner of the photograph. "Are you sure? Why are you so sure?" she asked.

I sat back and cleared my throat. "The man you thought was him is a decoy. He moves too fast and arrives at the painting each day at the same time. He never looks at anything else. It's too obvious. When he gets in front of the painting, he's not even studying it. See this picture here?" I said as I held it to Eloise's face. "He's glancing down to check his watch. He was only in the room for two minutes. Why does he need to check his watch?"

"We didn't notice that. That is strange." Eloise said as she studied the pictures more intently. She peered up from a photograph and asked, "Why do you think this is him? I can only make out the back of his head." She continued to stare at the picture as if it would somehow unfold itself to her.

"The decoy goes out of his way each day to walk by that person on the bench." My fingers moved across the picture. "He acknowledges the other man, who does not even move a muscle. He wants us to focus on the decoy." I pointed at the figure on the bench. "That person is sitting on the only seat in the entire gallery where the cameras don't show his face. Also, a man wearing those clothes is not in any of these photos from the lobby or the other areas of the museum. Each day, the same clothes, but no pictures coming in or going out. He knows the gallery, he knows the cameras, and he is hiding in plain sight."

Eloise put the pictures down and folded her hands. "Very good, but what does this tell us?"

"It tells us that he's still in Paris and that he's still here for *Blue No. 2*." My triumph soon faded as I blurted out, "But why did he steal our recipes? It doesn't make any sense."

Eloise pushed back into her chair. "Ah yes, the recipes. Our sources tell us that his negotiation with a certain Madame Fontaine stalled, and he's now shopping them elsewhere. It is not his style—just selling stolen goods. It's rather boring for him, don't you think?"

She was right about that. The Red Fox was known for his grandiose public displays, not private dealings. "He is a thief. Perhaps it *is* only for the money," I muttered as my attention switched back to Father.

"Maybe, but for now let's remain focused on the Chocolatiers' Ball. That will be the perfect time for our fox to surface. You will be there with your father?" Eloise asked.

My eyes lifted off the photos. "Yes, of course. I'll be helping him prepare for the rest of the week. That evening, I can stay close to the painting and keep an eye out."

"Our agents will be in the room, and I will be there as well," Eloise said as she brushed her desk off. "I have not been to a ball in years. Have you picked out your dress?"

My heart began to race, and my eyes opened as big as saucers. "A dress?" I hadn't even considered what I would wear.

What am I going to do? I thought. But my panic was soon gone, as I had the perfect solution. "The V," I whispered.

I can still hear the thunderous screaming from the phone receiver as I placed it back on the stand. Needless to say, the V would accompany me to shop for a dress. I had never shopped for a dress before, much less a ball gown. Mother had bought me Sunday dresses before, but I had some direction: nothing fancy, no sparkles, and nothing girly. The V would be at the store in 18 minutes.

"I assume the V will be here soon?" Father asked as he glanced up from a bowl of milk chocolate.

"Yes, in a few minutes," I replied as I straightened my right cuff. I knew the V would be over as soon as possible. Maybe 13 minutes if she tried.

Father started to wipe his hands and said, "I know dresses are not exactly your thing, but this is important to me. We need to show them all that the LaFrays are back. Confidence! That's what we need to project, confidence." I could tell that he was trying to reassure himself with this gesture, but that was fine. Above all, I wanted him to be happy.

"Whatever you pick, have them bill me. Monsieur Marcel is an old friend, and I'm sure he'll be helpful," Father said with rising confidence. He was now mixing a variety of chocolates in a larger silver bowl and smelling the aroma. "Be home by 6:30. We still have much to discuss about our entry."

"Of course, by 6:30," I replied.

The front door flew open with such force you would have thought the V was being chased. She had made it in just over eight minutes. Panting, she said, "I got here as soon as I could." She took several breaths. "I just can't believe it." She panted some more. "We're going dress shopping!"

Father gave a nod to us as we walked out the door. "Be back by 6:30! Perhaps you can join us for dinner tonight, V." The door had closed behind us before he could finish.

The V's mouth was moving a mile a minute. She was perhaps the most worldly 12-year-old in Paris. Halfway down the block, she stopped in her tracks and turned to me. "It's Marcel's; it has to be Marcel's."

For a split second I felt like most 12-year-old girls would have felt. A smile warmed my face, and I replied, "Of course, Marcel's." The V squealed and clapped her hands as we ran to the bus stop. The entire city was now open to us.

For me, walking up to Marcel's Couture was akin to the first time I had been ice skating. It was uncomfortable, potentially dangerous, and by all measure utterly foreign. The V led the way. The plate-glass doors were set in heavy polished brass frames that were flanked by large stone urns billowing with flowers and boxwoods. The sidewalk was swept and the glass store windows crystal clear and flawless, with perfectly dressed mannequins drawing you in.

The V grabbed my hand, and we opened the doors together. Three steps down polished marble stairs delivered us into the foyer. The V strutted about as if she owned the place. My eyes wandered to take it all in. We were centered on a large red Persian rug with a chandelier the size of a flying saucer hanging overhead. The walls were lined with fabric panels, displays, and cascading flower arrangements with a large runner leading into the grand salon. The air was fragrant with flowers and soft perfume. The glass doors slowly shut behind us, and two figures approached. It was time to lace up my skates.

"Mademoiselle LaFray! Your father said you would be stopping by," said the impeccably dressed man as he approached us with his arms outstretched. Marcel St. Moet was a legend in Paris.

He had been the founder and head designer of the world-famous l'Homme fashion house, but later sold it to return to what he loved most—couture dresses. The store had been open for nine years and was by appointment only—and, a few days ago, was the last place I would have thought I might be. His warm personality filled the great salon, and we were completely at ease. *How does he do that?* I wondered. Walking behind him holding a notebook was a young woman with silky black hair swept up in a knot.

"Bonjour! Bonjour and welcome to my store, Mademoiselles," Marcel said in grand fashion as he stepped into the foyer.

The V stepped forward without hesitation. "I am Mademoiselle Cantone, although you can call me V. This is Simone." The V appeared to hug herself and twirled while saying, "She's here for a ball gown."

"Oh, I see," Marcel replied with a large smile. "Well, it is a pleasure to have you both in my boutique." He paused, "Ah yes, Mademoiselle Cantone. How is your mother? I have not seen her in weeks."

The V's eyes were already racing forward into the salon like a kid in a candy shop. "She's fine," the V replied.

"And I would like to introduce my assistant. This is Bridget and she will be helping you today."

"Bonjour, girls," Bridget said as she stepped forward and shook our hands.

"I'm very lucky to have her, and right out of design school," Marcel added.

Immediately I liked Bridget. She was in her early twenties with perfect skin, large brown eyes, and a radiant smile. Her clothes and shoes were expensive, although she made them look comfortable and understated. Her dress was light linen with embroidered roses at the waist, and her shoes were black polished leather with just enough heel and point at the toes. In my business, I can pick out an imposter in an instant, but there was absolutely nothing fake about her. She looked down at her notebook, wrote something, and looked up. "So, ladies, shall we get started?" I turned and took one last look at the door. There was no turning back now. Time to toe the ice.

We followed Marcel and Bridget down another three steps into the grand salon. Chandeliers spanned the ornate ceiling in all directions, and the white marble walls were lined with gilded mirrors, framed fashion sketches, and racks of dresses. Enormous Persian rugs covered the highly polished marble floors with large sofas and fitting stands placed about. Classical music and the intoxicating smell of fresh-cut flowers filled the air as I spun to take it all in. It was like no place I had ever been before.

"Ladies," Marcel bellowed, clearing his throat. "You are in good hands with Bridget. I will be back shortly," he said as he disappeared behind some curtains.

"See something you like?" Bridget asked me with a warm smile as she ran her hands across a rack of dresses. The pit in my stomach returned for just a second, and I counted every hanger on the rack. There were 16 dresses on this rack. Bridget could tell that I was uneasy and said, "Oh, we have. more. Now go into that dressing room, and I will pull a few you might like."

The curtain closed behind me as a stared at myself in a full-length mirror. "What are you doing here?" I whispered to myself.

Suddenly, the V's head poked through the curtain. "Isn't this place fabulous?"

I looked back at the mirror and smiled. "Yeah, it's great."

A few minutes later, Bridget pulled back the curtain slightly and asked, "Are you ready?" My knees wobbled, but I was moving forward. "I have several for you to try."

I took one last look in the mirror and replied, "Ready as I'll ever be."

Bridget swept in and hung an armful of dresses on a rack. "I believe these are your size, dear," she said while removing one. "Ah yes, this dress is beautiful," she said as she displayed it in front of me. It was a pale purple, sleeveless ball gown with a dark purple sash. The skirt was fine lavender lace over white toile, and it had something puffy under it. I stared at it for a moment.

"Well? What do you think?" Bridget asked, moving the dress slightly from side to side.

"I'm going to put *that* on?" I replied.

Two minutes later, the zipper was up, and my hair was in my face. I looked like a purple cream puff that had somehow been deflated of cream. It was a disaster.

"Are you coming out?" screamed the V from outside the dressing room.

Bridget walked out and made the announcement. She cleared her throat. "May I introduce dress number one."

Against my better judgement, my right sock pushed through the curtain, and I stepped out.

"Ahhhh!" the V screamed with her hands on her cheeks. "It's perfect! Don't you think?"

I was trying to feel comfortable even though it was itchy and the skirt was heavy. "I don't know, V. Let's try another." And I was back behind the curtain in a flash.

Bridget walked in behind me. "That's a beautiful dress, Simone, but for some reason I don't think it's you. Let's try on the next one."

After helping me change, Bridget emerged again into the salon to make the announcement with the V waiting intently. "May I introduce dress number two," she said, and she pulled back the curtain. This dress was gray and boring compared to the other. It had a stiff taffeta skirt, and the top was thick with an embroidered pattern. The skirt was poofy and you could also see my knee caps.

"No, I don't think that's it," said the V. "The other one is much better," she added while reclining on a chair, and back behind the curtain I went.

Bridget stepped through the curtain holding a new dress. "I've been holding this one back," she said, hanging it on the rack. I could sense that my skates were about to fly out from under me, and I would soon be hitting the ice. Was it too late to dash out?

Bridget stepped back and smiled. "I'll be right back," she said and, in a flash, she returned with a shiny shoe box. "Now let's try this dress on." She unzipped the bag, pulled it out, and turned slowly.

"Wow," I whispered. The dress was pale pink with an A-line toile skirt that floated to the floor. It was sleeveless with a V-neck top and jeweled sash. Light reflected off tiny sparkles in the skirt. It was the most magnificent dress ever.

"Arms up," Bridget said.

The dress slipped on easily and was a perfect fit. It felt like nothing I had ever worn.

"Let's try on these shoes," Bridget said as she placed a pair of sequined, heeled shoes on the floor. They didn't have much of a heel, but I had never worn shoes like this. She helped me slip them on, and I felt a meter taller. "Oh, Simone," Bridget gasped, pulling my hair back. "Take a look."

I turned slowly to face the mirror and tried not to stumble. This was it. With my eyes open, a warm feeling poured over my body. The gown looked like it was made just for me.

"Beautiful," I whispered.

"Come on, Simone; even Marcel is out here waiting," the V groused from outside.

"Yes, mademoiselle. We don't have all day," Marcel added.

Bridget went back out to the salon for the announcement. "May I introduce to you the princess of the Chocolatiers' Ball," she said.

I stepped out with hair back, glasses off, and full confidence—the V fell to her knees. Marcel dropped his tea cup on the floor. They were speechless. I twirled softly and said, "I think this is the one."

"Mademoiselle! I just don't know what to say—you are simply exquisite," said Marcel as he realized his cup had shattered. The V squealed and said, "We'll take it! And the shoes, too."

That evening, after everyone was asleep, I sat on my bed, staring at the dress hanging in the corner. It looked like it was floating in the air. I glanced down, and the screen on my laptop read *Connecting*. In a flash it came to life, and I nearly squealed myself when I saw her face. "Mother, you won't believe what happened today."

21.9 Kilos

That was my best night of sleep in weeks, curled up in my blanket with the city air moving over me. I was deep in a dream when the sound of a banging garbage truck echoed down the alley. This was not my preferred way to wake up, but for some reason I found it oddly comforting. Optimism for the day ahead poured over me with one big stretch. The ball was only one day away, and my mother would be home soon.

All through breakfast, Mia whined and complained about missing the ball. "Why can't I go? You don't even like stuff like that. Can you ask Father if I can go?" She persisted while getting dressed and even while walking downstairs. It was exhausting.

Father had been in the kitchen since 3:30 a.m. He and I agreed to assemble the final entry Saturday morning for delivery, but he had grown impatient. As I tied my apron and tucked a few loose strands of hair under my cap, I turned to find him crafting the final touches.

"That wasn't the plan," I muttered, but I was encouraged by his drive. This was the man I knew.

"Wow!" I whispered.

Covered in chocolate and full of energy, Father shouted, "What do you think? The Plaza de Toros has never looked so delicious. Carmen herself would have to take a bite."

"The Plaza de what?" Mia asked, circling around.

The chocolate creation was heavy in scale, with all the appointments of a bull-fighting arena. Spectacular, with detail and decadence over every square centimeter. Mia's mouth fell open in amazement, and I concluded that it likely weighed 21.9 kilos and contained more than 20 varieties of chocolate and fudge. Dark chocolate, milk chocolate, white chocolate, raspberry-infused chocolate, and on and on. The smell was intoxicating, and every angle showed a new detail. It was a masterpiece.

"It looks great, Father," I said as my eyes continued to study it.

"I have a few more characters and—and I must shave some more chocolate to dust the ring floor with, but it's nearly finished. I was up all night putting it together," Father added. "Oh, I almost forgot—I still have a few more pieces in the freezer."

Father opened the small walk-in and grabbed a few flat trays. He had kept all of the pieces cold before assembly and planned to move the entire piece back into the freezer before delivery. While gazing at one of the outer walls and pushing my glasses back, I observed some water beads forming on the chocolate surfaces, although they were small.

"I don't think that's a big deal," I muttered.

"Your dress, dear, tell me about your dress," Father asked, to Mia's dissatisfaction, while re-emerging from the freezer.

"Why can't I go? She doesn't even like stuff like that. I should go. I should have bought a new dress," Mia huffed, her arms crossed.

"Well, I see that you have some definite opinions on this, Mia," Father responded in a low voice. While giving her a hug, he offered, "Maybe next time, baby girl. I would take you if I could, but the invitation is for myself plus one. I'm sorry, but Simone needs to be there. Besides, we need you here in case Mother gets home early."

Mia's sulking demeanor quickly changed to joy. "Mom is coming home? Yeah! I have so much to tell her about. Where is she? When is she coming home? Come on, Gigi, let's go straighten our room. Mother does not like it messy," she said, and in a flash she raced up the stairs.

For the next half hour, we went over every detail of the entry.

I hung on every detail, attempting to rebuild my lost confidence. *This can't be the work of a fraud,* I said to myself over and over again. We finished the last few details and took two steps back. It was finished.

"It's magnificent, Father," I said reassuringly.

Father went on about the arrangements with the delivery service and then started to clean up. I grabbed the broom and relished his excitement—it was palpable. Typically, I would tune these things out, but every word brought normalcy back to the store.

It was bizarre to have the store empty on a Friday morning, but I could not help but feel my world returning. From time to time, customers would peer in the window—all familiar faces trying to catch a glimpse of the action inside. As I put away the last of the pans and hung up the apron, the back door opened slowly.

"Hello, Louie," Uncle Giles said, pulling a file out of his briefcase. His eyes were drawn to the display. "What is this?" he asked with a slightly raised voice. He moved toward the table with a look of utter amazement. "Louie, this must have taken you days to prepare."

"About two days altogether," Father responded with pride in his voice. "I don't know if I could do it again."

Giles righted himself and glanced over at me. "Hello, Simone. I would assume that you have been very busy as well? You must be very proud."

What? I thought. *Was that a compliment?* I was not sure what to say. "Yes, sir. Father has been working very hard." As I turned to secure the apron on its peg, I noticed my watch blinking.

Giles peered over. "Do you have an appointment?" he asked.

Caught by surprise, I said, "I think there might be something wrong with it. Sometimes it just—maybe it needs a new battery."

Giles continued to stare a second longer and then turned to discuss business with Father.

"Father, I'm going to check on Mia. I hope she is not trying to straighten my room, too."

"Certainly, Simone," Father replied. "Don't take too long. I still need your help down here."

"Of course, it will only take a minute," I said, making my way to the stairs. "I hope Eloise has good news," I whispered.

Mia and Gigi were setting up for a tea party when I entered. Mia had just peeled an orange, and the aroma was all through the room. They were using it as their snack. "Mom will be home soon, and there is nothing she likes better than a tea party. Maybe you can come if you are not too tired from your ball," Mia said, folding paper towels into napkins.

"I'll be in my room for a minute," I said as I walked by.

The computer connected almost immediately, and there was Eloise in a crisp white shirt and navy blazer. She got right to the point. "Simone, we have much to discuss. First, *Blue No. 2* safely arrived at the galleria. The normal precautions have been made, including a posted guard. We are certain that he will be in the room tomorrow night. Our intelligence tells us that the recipes are still being offered to a select group of buyers and that he is planning some type of stunt during the ball. It is the perfect venue for his—antics." Eloise paused a second to read a piece of paper that had been handed to her.

She glanced up. "Simone, I fear that there may be some attempt to embarrass your father, and we will do everything we can to stop it. Not to worry. Myself and at least eight other agents will be in the room. If you see anything funny, *anything*, let us know immediately. We will take it from there. Get some rest tonight, Simone. Tomorrow is going to be a big day."

"I'll be ready," I replied somberly. "I'll see you there."

When I got back to the kitchen, Giles had gone, and Father was basking in the sweet smell of his creation. I was slightly alarmed to see that more drops were beading along the various surfaces, but it would be back in the freezer soon.

"Did Uncle Giles go out the front door?" I asked.

"What? Ah, yes, I think so. No—maybe the back."

I noticed that the front door was half open, which struck me as odd, but what I saw through the glass to the left was simply startling. The Fox was back. Though he stood between two patrons and was thinly disguised in a hat and glasses, I was sure that it was him.

"It's him!" I muttered as I tapped the emergency code on my watch.

As I ran toward the door, I could faintly hear Eloise's voice saying, "What is it, Simone? What's going on?" There was no time to talk.

Father looked up to see what was going on and yelled, "Simone? What is it?"

The Fox saw me dodging through the store and quickly stepped toward the open front door. As I slid under the counter, he pulled the door shut with a thunderous *SLAM* that reverberated throughout the store.

I stopped in my tracks and turned around. Two spatulas fell off the side of the table and then a pan. The rack above was still clanging as my eyes moved downward. Father's elaborate chocolate creation sat there as if on a precipice. In the next second, the near corner of the Plaza de Toros slumped, then the back. Then, the magnificent confection collapsed on itself, half of it splattering across the floor. It was ruined.

I brought my watch up to my face. "I'll call you later." I gasped.

Father turned to fully take in what had happened. Shoulders and head slung, mouth open. All of the confidence and excitement that had been exuding from him only seconds earlier had now vanished. He raised his hand to push the hair back from his face. "It can't be—it can't be. I'm ruined."

For the next several minutes, we stared at the heap in shock. There was nothing to salvage, and I again searched for something to say, but nothing was right. What can you say to someone who just watched his dream shattered? The silence was broken by three knocks at the back door. A man shouted, "Moving company!"

After telling the men that there would be no delivery to the galleria today, Father closed the door and leaned into it. "What are we going to do, Simone? It took me two days to make it, and the ball is tomorrow. I don't have enough ingredients for one truffle."

"It's going to be OK. We will figure something out," I offered while putting my arm around him.

As these words left my mouth, anger welled up inside me. *Why is he doing this?* I thought. Anger was not a familiar emotion, but it was building freely, and I had no intention of reining it in. Now fuming, I stared over at a thin pastry rolling board that was standing in a drying rack. Without thinking and with no reservation, I made a fist and chopped it into two clean pieces.

With all clouds lifted and my rage vanished, I stared into my father's eyes and said confidently, "We're going to do this, and it's going to be even better." Without blinking I said, "You are going to make an ingredient list. We are going to start working now, and we will make the best chocolate display that the world has ever seen. We can do this."

Father stared at me for a minute, and then a sliver of confidence reflected back at me. Without a word being said, he slid over the trash can, and I started to pick up the rolling board's pieces of wood.

"You need to start on that list—now," I said.

"A list. Ah yes—ingredients. Can you get me a pen and paper from the desk? Is your hand OK?" The enormity of what we were about to start sunk in, but it did not matter. We had no choice. "I am going to need your help," Father said.

Without losing eye contact, I replied, "Of course, now let's get going on that list."

For the remainder of the day and into the wee hours of the night, we collaborated on what was to become a true masterpiece. I focused on the temperature, weight, and structural assembly, while Father designed, mixed, baked, and sculpted his finest work. While the display now residing in the trashcan was monolithic and stoic, this display was a collage of scenes that spiraled upward. The town plaza, the Spanish countryside, a bull, and even the cigarette factory were intertwined with scrolling musical staffs, clef notes, and other notations in precise detail. Every type of chocolate and fudge we could put our hands on was put to use; no detail spared, no shortcut taken. The first display may have been magnificent, but this one—this one was art.

We talked the entire time and took no breaks, except to feed Mia and tuck her into bed. I caught Father staring at me twice, as if I had grown up in front of him that day, and I had rediscovered who he really was—my father, the man who knew how to work magic with sweets while providing unconditional love and guidance to his daughters. We both fell asleep in the kitchen that night, pans and ingredients everywhere, and woke to the sound of the paper hitting the front door. The Chocolatiers' Ball was only hours away.

The Bag with No Label

*D*rip—*drip*—*drip* resonated from the kitchen sink as the saucepans took a much-needed break. It was music to my ears—the remnants of a prolific evening that culminated in the production of the most glorious confection ever created. The store was right again, Father could do no wrong, and I was sinking back into the shadows. He now had the lead, and I could concentrate on la Volpe Rossa. Father put the final touches on his masterpiece and, finally, it was done. The imagination, the size, the detail, the sweet smell, all in a glorious concert, but it was Father who now stood above it all. At that moment, my only wish was for time to stand still, but there was much to do.

After feeding Mia and wrestling with my wardrobe for something clean and serviceable, it was time to call in. Eloise would have my final briefing for the evening, and perhaps Mother was on her way home.

After we finished going over the room, the program, and the operatives to be engaged, Eloise said, "I've uploaded all the drawings and contact information into your phone. The trap is set. We just need a willing thief."

"I'm ready, Eloise," I said with complete conviction.

"I have no doubt of that. See you tonight," she replied, signing off.

"Ah, wait!" I said to her. "Is Mother on her way home?"

Eloise's eyes refocused on me, and a slight hesitation moved over her brow. "Soon, dear, she's in a bit of a spot right now, but soon. Maybe late tonight."

"Right," I whispered to myself.

Turning away from the wardrobe, I caught a glimpse of the dress hanging on the closet door. In the morning light, it was magical. The light perfectly hitting the sequins caused long glimmers to illuminate the room. You would think it was floating. The material was soft and light as I ran my fingers over it on my way out of the room. There was still much to do.

"Simone!" Father boomed up from the kitchen. "The delivery men will be here any minute. Please hurry! I need your help with something."

The door had just closed behind me, and I was midway down the steps. I found Father meticulously going over the sides of the structure, and thankfully no water was beading. He checked the clock on the wall and then his own watch. "They will be here in about five minutes," he said with growing nervousness. "Simone, I need to get something from the apartment. Can you keep an eye on things?"

"Of course, Father," I replied. "I'll clean up. Go on."

I began collecting empty wrappers and other bits of paper, inspecting each one before tossing it in the trash can. There was not an ounce of chocolate left; every ingredient in the store had been used. The bags looked to be in order, but—

"What's this?" I murmured. One bag had been stuffed under the wooden table, but the label had been removed. At first glance it looked like a sugar bag—the smell, the texture—but at that moment, a loud knock came from the back.

"Here for pickup!" someone shouted from the other side of the door.

Immediately a voice traveled down the stairwell, and when I looked up, Father's head appeared in the apartment door. "Let them in, Simone, but don't let them touch anything before I get there!" His head ducked back into the apartment.

"Of course, Father. I'll have them wait for you." My mind went back to the bag for a second. *Probably nothing. Maybe the label just came off*, I thought on the way to the door.

Behind the door were two burly men in denim coveralls and caps.

"Good morning," the shorter one said. "We have a pick-up order for Monsieur LaFray," he added.

"Yes, one minute please," I replied with my arm around the door to expose my watch. I was taking no chances today and quickly sent a picture of them off to the ministry. Eight seconds later, my screen illuminated a soft green.

"Good," I whispered. "Please come in. He will be along in just a minute."

"Wow!" they said in unison as their eyes wandered over the structure. "Is that it?"

"Yes, that's it," I replied and turned to them. There was something I had to say.

"Monsieurs, may I suggest that you take Rue Tele to Morida, and then straight down Rue de LaFleur until you get to the round-about. From there make a left on Ruran, then right into the alley. From there, it is the seventh door on the right. There should be plenty of unloading space."

They stared, and then the taller man said with a chuckle, "Thanks for the advice, mademoiselle, but we're taking our way starting with Rue Clarion, then—"

No, no, no, I thought and quickly cut him off. "Your way may be shorter, but Rue Clarion is having repairs, and most of the roads from there on are lined with potholes. This is a very delicate delivery, and the trip needs to be as smooth as possible. Please take it under advisement."

"Gentlemen," Father said as he burst from the stairs. "This is very precious cargo. Our route must have as little turbulence as possible."

"I believe we have it covered, sir," one of them said to him while the other winked at me.

For the next 20 minutes, Father meticulously loosened the display board and took endless measurements to make sure it would fit into the van. He also checked the interior of the van, and then it was finally time to move it. The men carefully lifted the display and started to inch their way out the door. I made sure that their path was clear and all doors were wide open. With a collective exhale, they placed the confection in the van and strapped it down. Father jumped in, and I glanced up and down the alley for any oncoming trucks.

Father stared at his masterpiece and said, "Simone, I'll ride along and make sure it gets there safely. When I'm done, I'll catch a bus home. We leave at 5:15, so you need to be dressed and ready by 5:00."

"5:00, of course, I'll be waiting," I replied.

Father gave an anxious smile, and the delivery man closed the doors. As they shut, my mind returned to the plain bag.

My fears were justified. My tongue confirmed that the bag with no label was indeed laced with salt. It was very fine and mixed into the sugar convincingly, but the taste was undeniable.

"*Oh no,*" I whispered. "There's salt in the chocolate. Maybe Father caught it?"

I went over the kitchen carefully, trying to find any unwashed bowls or spoons to sample, but they had all been washed. There was no way to know for sure, but that uneasy feeling was starting to come back. For the next two hours, I finished cleaning and then took Gigi for a walk. I needed the fresh air as much as she did.

When we returned to the store, Mia was sitting at the front table wearing her best dress, party shoes, and Sunday hat. "I am ready for the ball," she announced as the door closed behind us. "I have decided that I'm part of this family, and I *like* fancy things. I have to go to the ball! Do you like my hat?"

I can't say that I was surprised.

"Mia, you know that both Father and I will be busy tonight, and we cannot watch you in such a large crowd," I replied. "Besides, Monsieur John and Madame Tris are looking forward to babysitting you. I believe they have the whole evening planned out. Madame Tris mentioned something about a tea party."

Mia relented. "Well, I do enjoy a tea party, but I want to go to the ball. You don't even like that kind of stuff." She started to twirl. "The dresses, the dancing, the champagne. It's too fancy for you."

"The champagne for sure, but Father needs me, and only two are invited—remember?" I could feel her disappointment and had a thought. "Hey, maybe you could give me some pointers on being fancy," I said.

Mia's eyes grew as big as saucers. As best I could recall, this was the first time I asked her to help with anything.

"Yes!" she squealed. For the next hour, Mia showed me how to walk fancy, talk fancy, and be fabulous. She was having the time of her life, but I could not take any more.

"OK, Mia—I got it, I got it."

"Should you need my services, I will be upstairs," Mia replied rather snootily.

There would have to be more salt somewhere, I thought as I moved back into the kitchen. I once again scoured every bowl, every surface, and every utensil, but nothing. Just two small shavings of chocolate under an empty bag. I was relieved to find that they tasted OK, but it was not enough. At this point, I could only wait and hope.

A key went into the back door's lock, and Father strolled in. "You won't believe it, Simone! The decorations, the lighting, the chocolate—everywhere you look is something more decadent than the next. And the displays! Steep competition." He collected himself and held out his arm. "Shall we get ready?" I dared not mention the bag of laced sugar. It was too late now.

Getting ready was more challenging than you would think, as I always dressed to be unseen. However, for this event, blending in meant dressing up. This was an event of pomp and finery that brought out some of the most flamboyant characters in Europe. *What have I gotten myself into?* I said to myself, putting on my glasses and pushing my hair into my face. I had noticed Mia peeking through the door, but she suddenly burst in.

"I simply can't let you go to the ball like this. What are you thinking?" she said with a brush and Mother's makeup bag in hand.

Father was pacing the floor and stewing over all the things that could go wrong when we entered.

"How do I look?" I asked sheepishly. In my entire life, I had never asked anyone this question.

Father stood up slowly as a single tear rolled down his face, and he smiled. "You're beautiful, Simone. Shall we go?"

The Chocolatiers' Ball

E ntering the Grand Palais Gallery was spectacular on an ordinary day, but this was no ordinary day. The entry hall was lined with flowers and confectioners' decorations, and overhead hung two large swags of intertwined ribbons suspending a series of candle-lit chandeliers. At the end of the hall on either side of the doors were two enormous crystal vases full of gum balls and ribbon candies that cascaded to the floor. The smell of chocolate and sweets was intoxicating.

"Have you ever seen anything like this?" Father asked me.

I paused for a second, fidgeted with my dress, and said, "No, it's absolutely unreal."

As we made our way through the grand hall, I counted two agents and saw Eloise past the vases having a conversation with someone in the galleria. She saw us coming from the corner of her eye. As we entered the main gallery room, we were asked to stop as a steward read our names aloud.

"Monsieur Louie LaFray and Mademoiselle Simone LaFray," he shouted.

In the next second, a man of some official capacity walked up to welcome us. "Bonjour, Monsieur LaFray," I heard him say as my mind trailed elsewhere. As they talked, I counted six more agents, and there hanging on the wall, to the side of Father's display, was *Blue No. 2*. Well-lit and perfectly level.

"Brilliant," I whispered to myself. They were only six meters apart.

"Bonjour, Louie. It is nice to see you," Eloise said as the man greeted the next guest.

Father adjusted his glasses, and I slipped my right foot out of the increasingly uncomfortable shoe to uncurl my toes. "Bonjour, Eloise, it is good to see you as well." He paused. "When should we be expecting Julia home?"

Without expression Eloise glanced away then said, "Perhaps this evening. Another mission accomplished, although she does have a long flight in front of her. Are you ready for your big night?"

"Yes, of course. Thank you for coming, but I must attend to my business now. Enjoy your evening, Eloise," Father said. As soon as he turned, another familiar face appeared.

"Good evening, Louie," said Uncle Giles.

What is he—? I started to think, but then remembered that he represented many patisseries in the city and was an ex-facto member of the International Federation of Chocolatiers. Their grandfather was a founding member, and many LaFrays had been members at some time or another.

"It should be a big night for you, Louie. Much to look forward to," Uncle Giles said as they shook hands.

It's time to go to work, I thought. "Father? Can I take a look around?"

"Of course, but don't be long," he replied. "Are you going to size up the competition?"

"Yes, something like that," I replied as I melted into the crowd.

The dress was now cooperating, although I found myself thirsty and headed for the refreshments. The room was crowded and loud, exactly how I wanted it. On my way, I passed the competition. It was the Pantheon of chocolatiers. Mauricio Braga, the South American Saint of Cocoa, was putting the final touches on a massive swirled chocolate shadow-box display of *The Marriage of Figaro*. Victor A. Petrov, the Czar of the Bar, had created mosaic panels of *The Magic Flute* with his delectable candy bars. Bo Cho, the Saucoress of Seoul, had arrived a week previously and had been working on her display, which was concealed behind a large curtain. Known for her decadent mousses and complex sauces, she was the returning champion with absolute certainty of a repeat. In the next second, flash bulbs went off as the curtain dropped to expose her hand-carved, dark-chocolate filigree display of *The Barber of Seville*. It was magnificent. And then, at the end was a multi-tiered, chocolate and flower-laden diorama of *Madam Butterfly*. It was massive in scale and could only be the work of one man, Hans Müller, the finest chocolatier in all Germany and perhaps the world. Simply known as "the Count," Müller was a culinary prodigy who had published four cookbooks by the age of 12 and opened his own chocolate factory at 14. He was quietly placing the final details on a pagoda when he noticed me studying his work. "*Was denken sie?*" he asked me.

"*Es ist erstaunlich. Viel glück,*" I replied as I walked away. This was not going to be easy.

The fruit punch hit the spot, although it occurred to me while taking my second gulp that it would stain my dress. While I was carefully pulling the glass away from my lips, the lights dimmed, and the program was called to order.

Seizing an opportunity to move through a calm room, I set the cup down, and off I went. I counted 642 guests, 16 band members, 32 staff, and 10 agents.

"Why do they all have to be wearing the same thing?" I groused, but my totals were right on. The crowd cheered at the conclusion of the announcements, and the music program began. The band rang out, and most of the guests started to dance around me.

By some minor miscalculation, I found myself in the middle of the dance floor. I turned to make my way out, saying,

"*Excusezmoi,*" when an older, rather short, gray-haired gentleman stepped in front of me.

"May I have this dance, mademoiselle?" he asked with an outstretched arm.

Stunned, but not looking to be rude, I nodded, and our waltz began.

I had taken dance class in the third grade, but it was nothing like this. We moved awkwardly at first, but by the end of the first bar, I was in perfect time. Gazing over the gentleman's shoulder, I tried to hold an eye on Father, although the movement and spinning complicated things. In fact, I started to feel dizzy and my dress was bunching, but the song was almost over. Only 28 seconds left.

"Thank you for the dance, and enjoy your evening," the man uttered while bowing and eyeing a potential partner behind me.

"Thank you," I sheepishly replied.

When I finally returned to our display, I could not help but think of the salt-laced sugar bag. It was once again dominating my thoughts. The room was again loud and rowdy as the band started into another song. Looking over the crowd, I noticed a pair of side doors open, and the panel of judges entered the room. Some sparse applause came in from the crowd, although most focus was on the dance floor. The judges proceeded to the first display with their scoring pads in hand. I couldn't take it any longer.

"Father? I have to talk to you about something."

Father was painstakingly going over every detail of the display, but he pushed his hair off his face and turned to me. "What's that? What is it, Simone?" he asked with squinting eyes.

I took a breath and very calmly said, "There was a discarded sugar bag under your counter with fine salt mixed in it. Do you use much salt in your recipes?"

Father stood up. "Salt? Well yes, a little, but—" he replied. I could tell that he was reworking the recipes in his head, but the chaos of the room was breaking his concentration. "I do remember finding a bag with no label, but—" he said, his confidence waning. I stared at him intently, blocking out all the noise around us. I processed his body language and every expressive detail of his face.

After three seconds, it was obvious. *Oh no*, I thought.

"It's fine," Father said. "I'm sure it's fine. Now can you help me place these figures?"

My heart sank, and the volume of the room returned. Something was very, very wrong.

I continued to watch Father intently, hoping to see glimmers that would change my mind. Busy and engaged, he spoke to onlookers and once again reveled in the experience.

"Maybe everything is OK," I murmured. The judges finished the first two displays and were making their way to the third. "It won't be long now," I whispered.

Suddenly, a rush of confidence bolted through me. *Wait a minute! Is this what he wants?* I quickly looked for *Blue No. 2* and it was still intact. *How could I get sidetracked like that? He's in the room, I know it.*

The agents were rotating their posts, and all appeared under control.

Eloise brushed by me and casually said, "Any minute now—something big is about to happen." She leaned in closer and whispered, "You need to get a better vantage point of the room. Perhaps the stage. You might get a better look from the stage."

She was right, and time was running short. Only 10 minutes now.

It was easy to perch myself in the shadows of stage right. The band played on, and *Blue No. 2* still hung untouched. As the music rose, my eyes moved back and forth across the crowd. "25 more people are in the room," I murmured. I was in my comfort zone. The judges were only one display away now, and a man stood in front of the painting. The height and build was right, and he hadn't moved in almost three minutes.

I raised my watch. "The man at the painting. Do we know him?"

Almost immediately, two agents moved in. He produced some credentials, which the agents scanned and returned.

A text message came back, "He checks out."

"Ugh. This dress," I whispered, fidgeting with the sash. My stomach started to churn as the judges finished evaluating the fourth display. The band stopped for their break and suddenly, it felt like I was the one being watched.

"Hello, Simone," said a soft voice from behind.

My body froze. It was *him*. La Volpe Rossa.

"Don't turn around. Keep looking forward—you'll want to see how this works out," he added. "I have to admit, I've never been entirely comfortable in formal situations. The privileged patting themselves on the back for their meaningless accomplishments. Rather boring, don't you think?" He paused a second, and my mind raced. "Cat got your tongue, Mademoiselle LaFray?"

His voice moved closer to me, but I was oddly unthreatened.

"Why are you doing this to us?" I asked confidently. "My father has never done anything to you. Why are you here?"

I could sense that he was moving from side to side.

"Ah yes, that is the question, isn't it? Why am I here?" he replied. "A series of coincidences, lucky gambles, and careful plans have brought us to this moment. It is no accident." He paused. "You believe I'm here to take something from you? Ah, you have much to learn, young Simone. Much to learn."

He paused for a second, then finally said, "You see, I am here for you, nothing else. You are the reason I'm here."

My mind went blank. "For me?" I whispered in disbelief. "What about our recipes? The painting?" I blurted out.

"Ah, the recipes," he said with a laugh. "The famous LaFray cookbooks—worth millions, I have been told, and that old painting. What to do with that? I guess some unfinished business there, but it's of no consequence."

For the first time in my life, I was confused because the facts were colliding. "Here for me?" I muttered again.

"The recipes proved to be helpful and the perfect distraction. I am confident that the real thief will be exposed shortly, but I certainly had no hand in that. Besides—recipes? Pah! Not my style."

He paused for another second, and his voice turned serious. "You are an extraordinary girl, Simone. A talent unparalleled, for sure, but you are surrounded by the wrong people. Dangerous and cruel people who do not have your best interests at heart." He paused again. "Several are even in this room. In time you will understand what I am saying, and it will be a hard pill to swallow, but the truth cannot be denied. The truth is always exposed."

I heard him take one step back, and my confidence bloomed. "Why are you telling me this? What cruel people?" I asked.

He interrupted. "Not enough time to explain tonight, dear, but I could not wait any longer. You have no idea how big your role will be, or even what is coming next." He paused and then whispered, "Enjoy the rest of your evening, Mademoiselle LaFray. I will be in touch."

And just like that, he was gone.

"Me? What role? What people?" I murmured as I gazed over the crowd and pulled my watch up to my face. "Eloise? Can you hear me?" I whispered.

"Yes, dear, what is it? You sound shaken," she replied.

"He's in the—" My voice stopped as I saw the judges nearing our display. "No time now; we'll talk later," I added. My mind was once again fixated on the laced sugar bag.

The three judges walked through the crowd with an unbridled arrogance. Each had medals dripping off their lapels, and two wore glasses that barely clung to their noses. The crush of the crowd was clearly irritating, although they pushed through with scoring sheets in hand. This was it.

From a distance, I could read their lips as they exchanged pleasantries, but I struggled to focus on the task at hand.

Here for me? Who stole the recipes? He must be lying, trying to distract me. There's no other possible answer, I said to myself as a troupe of performers took the stage.

Stagehands were adjusting the lighting and placing props when a lady placed a box full of costumes next to me and said, "You need to be moving along now, dear. The next act is on in five minutes. By the way, your dress is beautiful."

"Oh, oh yes," I replied as I slid to the side. Father was still visible and holding his own, although a large crowd had formed around him. The judges meticulously observed, measured, and even smelled Father's creation, all the time feverishly writing on their notecards. This went on for the next several minutes as Father looked on.

"This is good," I whispered. I could see Father's confidence growing. The judges huddled and entered into a fierce debate. The crowd closed in even further to hear their exchange.

"What is going on?" I whispered as I readjusted my sash again.

One judge appeared so upset that he had to sit down to collect himself.

"Turn around," I murmured, as I could not see what they were saying.

After several more tense minutes of conversing among themselves, the portly judge made a few final notes and approached Father. He was in plain view, and, luckily, he did not have a mustache to cover his mouth. I focused in.

"Monsieur LaFray, we will taste the samples now."

The request threw Father off-guard, although he gripped a long knife and cut several chunks.

My darkest fear was coming true. My father, who is everything good and stable in the world, was seconds from being publicly embarrassed and labeled as a fraud. Everything that I had accepted as my foundation was about to vanish before my eyes.

"This can't happen," I whispered.

The judges were inspecting the pieces now. The whole truth was inevitable—I had to do something.

The judges moved the chocolates under their noses, readying themselves to take their bites. At that moment, all the fear, all the emotion, all the weight of the recent happenings vanished, and I knew exactly what to do.

No more hiding, I said to myself as I walked to the middle of the stage, turned on the microphone, and took a deep breath. I could see the judges take their first bites.

As it would later be described to me, only those who were in attendance that evening could even begin to describe what happened over the next four minutes and 23 seconds. Most in the room had heard "Habanera" at some point in their lives, but what they witnessed was not only the singing of a song, but a performance so clear, so beautiful, and so mesmerizing that they could only describe it as—perfection.

I began the first verse with no accompaniment to a room overcrowded with noise. An ease came over me as I stood, completely exposed in the spotlight. Within seconds, those closest to the stage turned toward me in silence. Shortly after, the band joined in, but at very low volume. It appeared that they too were trying to hear me.

My voice grew in confidence, and my eyes fixated on the judges. They were still tasting and chewing as I started the second verse. In the next minute, even the judges were listening. I pushed through; this was the moment. There was no going back now. Many in the crowd held their hands clutched over their hearts, hanging on every word. One judge dropped his plate, which shattered on the floor, and even Father, who only minutes ago was agonizing over his current misfortune, mouthed each word with a loving gaze.

When I finished the last note, the room was perfectly still. All eyes in the crowd hung on me, begging for one more note, but I simply bowed and walked off into the shadows. As if cold water had been thrown over the audience, all those in attendance realized what they had witnessed, and they erupted into applause.

Backstage, I stood and listened. My entire life, I had taken comfort in being unnoticed, worked to avoid attention, and happily accepted silence, but tonight—tonight I was heard, and I loved it.

As I made my way back to Father's display, one of the judges passed by on his route to the podium. As I neared our display, the crowd parted as several recognized me from the stage.

"This will take some getting used to," I murmured, as all eyes were on me now. I guess that was how Mia felt.

Father stood there with open arms. "Simone? I didn't know. How did you—?" he said as the portly judge addressed the room from the stage's podium.

"Please! Can we all settle down? We have an announcement."

"This is it," Father said nervously, but it didn't matter. We were going to face this together.

"May we have your attention, please?"

The judge paused to place his glasses level on his face and straighten his jacket. He coughed. "We—the judges—have conferred, and we have a most extraordinary announcement. Tonight we have witnessed something inexplicable, and the purveyor must be exposed immediately."

He pointed to Father and said, "You, Monsieur LaFray. Your display is well done and, dare I say, spectacular, but your chocolate!" The judge paused. "Your chocolate, sir, is the best we have ever tasted. Bravo, Monsieur LaFray! We have conferred, and you are the winner. Bravo, sir!"

"We did it!" Father said to me as the crowd erupted in applause. He stood proudly, and one of the judges grasped our hands and thrust them into the air. As I adoringly stared at Father, the weight of the world was lifted, it all made sense again, and he was exactly who I hoped he was.

With a sense of formality, another judge walked up to us and presented an oversized blue ribbon and a written proclamation.

Then a figure burst from the crowd.

"No! No! It cannot be! He is a fraud!"

"I knew it," I whispered.

Bonjour

"So it was you," I said as Giles emerged from the crowd. The crowd hushed and turned all eyes to him. Swelling with emotion, Giles began to heave and wring his hands. He was furious, ready to erupt as he began to pace back and forth.

"His entire life, Louie has been graced by the recipes of our great-great-grandfather. He has no real talent! My father was the rightful heir to those recipes. He wanted to open a factory and expand the business. My uncle was no businessman, but our grandfather saw it differently. He always favored your father, Louie. Our grandfather selfishly gave the recipes away to the least deserving. Gave them to *him*! They have always been as much mine!" He now circled the display and pointed a finger viciously at Father.

"Giles? What's going—?" Father started to say.

But Giles was not in a listening mood. "Just like your father, Louie, you have floundered and pilfered away this fortune. I have offers of more than a million euros for these recipes!" Giles paused for a second. "You are not a great chocolatier! I mixed salt into your ingredients for days, and you had no idea. No idea at all! My father, now *he* was a great chocolatier!" Giles paused for a second, and then focused on Father.

"He does not deserve this—I do!" Giles shouted as he lunged at Father.

While Giles was still in midair, two guards tackled him to the ground and placed him in handcuffs. Eloise looked on sternly, talking into her watch.

"We'll take it from here, madam," the guard said as they

brought Giles to his feet. Eloise nodded and gave me a wink.

With the crowd still in disbelief over what had just happened, Father walked over to his cousin. He expression was bewildered. "Giles, how could you have done this? I didn't know. Why didn't you say something?" he said

Giles gave no reply, still writhing with anger like a caged animal.

"Take him away," Eloise ordered.

Father looked at me, still in disbelief, although the moment quickly vanished. Several onlookers said to me, "You're that girl! Where did you get that voice?" I had almost forgotten.

As the ball drew to a close, I watched Father continue to greet friends and bask in the moment. Our display had just set a record at auction, and life as I knew it had been restored. However, something was new; something was different. I was living in the moment—no more hiding. Father was happy and looked as if the weight of the world had been lifted from his shoulders. As I started to pack his utensils, an agent walked over and whispered in my ear. My joy was short-lived.

"What's that?" I whispered back, then took a look for myself.

It was true: *Blue No. 2* was gone!

The remainder of that evening passed in an instant, and I soon found myself slumped over the kitchen table picking at two eggs and a slice of toast. Gigi was front and center, staring up with an optimistic wag to her tail. Sunlight was starting to fill the apartment, and a lack of sleep stifled my energy.

Father had left the morning paper on the table with the metro section on top. The headline read, "FONTAINE PAYS RECORD €10,000 FOR LAFRAY DISPLAY AFTER MYSTERY THIEF EXPOSED!" But my eyes were drawn down to the headline under the fold that read, "MYSTERY GIRL CAPTIVATES CHOCOLATIERS' BALL"

"What have I done?" I whispered as Gigi's attention was pulled to footsteps from down the hall.

Mia had emerged from her bedroom with a particularly unruly mane of hair.

They must have been playing dress-up, I thought to myself.

Mia pushed her hair out of her face. "Can I eat some cereal before church? I'm sooooo tired. We stayed up late playing games and then—" She paused as her mind awoke. "The ball! How was the ball? Did you see any famous people? What happened? Tell me everything," she squealed, now perched directly in front of me.

I smiled and said, "Father is letting us sleep in today, so no church."

"Oh? So why are you up?" she replied without blinking.

"Couldn't sleep. Why don't you go back to bed, and I'll tell you all about it later."

Mia developed a stale look on her face as her hair had once again collapsed over her eyes. Midway down the hall, she froze and turned. "Is Mother home?" she asked.

"No, not yet," I replied, to her displeasure. "But soon. Hopefully before lunch."

"Great!" she replied. "I have so much to talk to her about."

"You and me both," I muttered, realizing my breakfast was now completely cold. "Why me? What does he want with me?" I whispered.

An hour later, Father was on a walk with Gigi, and I was in the store, cleaning the displays, as a well-dressed couple stopped to look through the front window. With hands cupped over their eyes, I could hear the gentleman say, "The paper said he won last night. I guess they will reopen this week."

Yes, we would be open that week, but life would not be the same. I was out in the open now—well, at least my singing was—and *Blue No. 2* was gone. There was absolutely no doubt in my mind that the Fox swiped it during Giles' outburst. It was as if he had known what was going to happen and seized on the opportunity. Smart. His words still rang through my head. "Here for me? What role am I going to play?" I whispered.

A high pitched "Aaaaaaah!" reverberated through the front glass as the V spotted me. She moved to the door, jumping up and down and talking a mile a minute.

"Hi V," I said as I unlocked and opened the door.

"Aaaaaaah!" she screamed again, hands on the side of her glasses. "Tell me everything! I heard you won. Did you win? And what is all this about Giles LaFray?" She paused to catch her breath as I placed some pastries on a plate for us to eat. Father had left these and a warm pot of tea before taking his walk.

The V pressed on: "I heard he freaked out and tried to kill you guys or something! Is that right? I can't believe it." She paused again. "Come to think of it, he is kind of creepy, all stuffy, and always looking down his nose."

I knew what was coming next.

The V stood up straight, and her face shifted as if she had a secret to tell. "And tell me about this mystery girl who is the talk of the town. Hmm."

"I—" I blurted out before being interrupted by Father and Gigi coming through the back door.

"Good morning, girls. Beautiful day out there. Did you hear the news, V? Apparently we are back. What a night!" he exclaimed. The leash went on the hook, and Gigi trotted to her water bowl.

The V turned to him. "I heard all about it. It's all everyone is talking about," she replied.

"Oh, it is, is it? You should have been there, V. It was a magical night. The crowd, the chocolate, the music!" Father paused and looked over at me. "Yes, a night full of surprises."

That's an understatement, I thought. While the V interrogated

Father for the next minute, my mind wandered back to the Red Fox. How had he known it was Giles all along, and what did he want with me? I was an analyst, not an operative.

"Simone? Simone? Are you with us?" Father asked.

"Oh yes, of course, just a little tired. What's that?" I replied.

"V was saying that there is a picture of you in the paper. I'll have to cut that out," Father said.

A picture? I was not used to having my picture taken, much less having it in the paper, but it didn't matter.

"How do I look?" came out of my mouth without a second thought. I couldn't believe I had said that again. Both Father and the V stared as smiles started to work across their faces.

"Bonjour, all!" Eloise said as she made her way through the front door. She was impeccably dressed and fresh for someone who had spent the previous evening in an interrogation room. "Quite an evening, wasn't it?" she asked, folding her coat over the back of a chair. "Congratulations are certainly in order, Louie, but I have much to tell you."

We all gathered around to hear what Eloise had come to say. She turned to Father. "Louie, Giles had been stealing from you for months, misreporting accounts, all in an attempt to swindle your business away."

"Ah," Father replied. "Giles did talk about partnering or possibly selling, but I just couldn't bring myself to consider it. Sell the store?"

"Yes," Eloise replied. "After you refused to sell it to him, frustration and greed got the best of him, so he stole your recipe books and tried to sell them to the highest bidder. Did you know he had a key to the store? Anyway, the books were all found in his office earlier this morning. Your cousin will be going away for some time." She looked at her watch quickly, then added, "You weren't the only one, Louie. He was stealing from most of his clients. We will be notifying them today."

"I still can't believe it," Father said. "Why didn't he just come to me? Harboring all those feelings. Julia's not going to believe this," he added. I had a feeling that Mother knew everything by now.

Eloise turned to me. "Simone? Can I have a word?"

I knew this was coming.

"Sure," said Father. "V. Can you help me in the kitchen?" Together, they exited the room.

Once we were alone, Eloise leaned in. "I'm guessing you have been pouring over what happened all night. We still don't know how he did it. The video flickered for just a second, and the painting was gone. It just vanished," she whispered.

"He talked to me when I was on the stage," I replied, and her eyebrow rose.

"Talked to you? Well, what did he say?" she replied with heightened curiosity.

"He—he told me that he was in Paris for me," I said.

Shock and disbelief ran over Eloise's face. "Here for you? What? I don't understand." She looked back and forth across the room and then over to me.

"How did he even know who you—?" Her face went blank, and she straightened her collar. "Did he say anything else?" she said, her tone turning stern.

"No, nothing else," I replied. This was the first lie I'd ever told Eloise. I was not proud of it, but I couldn't tell her. Not now. I was going to have to resolve that for myself.

"Eloise?" Father said from the kitchen. "I have cookies coming out of the oven and a pot of tea on. Would you like to join us?"

Eloise took another long look at me, then her demeanor softened. "That sounds perfect, Louie. Can I help?" she replied.

Father walked toward me, wiping his hands as Eloise prepared the tea. He put his hand on my cheek and said, "You reminded me of something critical these last few days. You reminded me of the strength of this family and who we are. Something I shouldn't have forgotten, but did. I am not proud of it, but I am overly proud of you. I could not have done this without you. Only you, Simone, could have helped me pull this off," he said.

With a dusting of flour on my cheek, I smiled back and said, "You're welcome." I paused. "It was quite a night, wasn't it?"

From the kitchen we heard Eloise say, "The tea is almost ready, and I forgot to tell you, Louie, your books will be returned later today."

"Ah!" Father said. "The recipe books." He looked at me and winked. "I don't know if we need them anymore."

The V and I laughed together, talking about dancing, dresses, our upcoming year at Trinity, and whether or not she could be my talent agent. She was negotiating hard.

"Your voice and my connections. Just think where we could go," she said, putting her arm over my shoulders.

"Ah, where *are* we going next?" I said to myself.

In the next instant, Mia darted by us with open arms. We heard the front door open, and the old bell rang. I sat straight up as if Christmas had suddenly fallen on me.

"Bonjour," said a welcome voice. Mother was home.

I still had much to sort out, but one thing was clear: my life was about to change. There was no going back now. No more hiding, but I was ready. At least I thought I was. No one could have predicted what was to come next—but that is another story.

FIN

S.P. O'Farrell wrote *Simone LaFray and the Chocolatiers' Ball* over the course of two and a half years after a particularly inspired bowl of bouillabaisse on a family vacation. The majority was written after all were tucked-in, the lights were low, and the mind was free to wander. Mr. O'Farrell lives in the northeastern United States with his wife Emily, sons Patrick and Michael, and their ever-dozing Labrador, Scout.